When a mystery writer abandons his typewriter to solve a real mystery, he'd better be prepared to deal with real cops, real corpses . . .

And real killers.

OUTSIDE IN

by the author of the
Albert Samson Mysteries
MICHAEL Z. LEWIN

Berkley books by Michael Z. Lewin

ASK THE RIGHT QUESTION
NIGHT COVER
OUTSIDE IN
THE SILENT SALESMAN
THE WAY WE DIE NOW

OUTSIDE IN

MICHAEL Z. LEWIN

BERKLEY BOOKS, NEW YORK

This Berkley book contains the complete
text of the original hardcover edition.
It has been completely reset in a type face
designed for easy reading, and was printed
from new film.

OUTSIDE IN

A Berkley Book / published by arrangement with
Alfred A. Knopf, Inc.

PRINTING HISTORY
Alfred A. Knopf edition / June 1980
Berkley edition / July 1981

ISBN: 0-425-05006-8

A BERKLEY BOOK ® TM 757,375
Berkley Books are published by Berkley Publishing Corporation,
200 Madison Avenue, New York, New York 10016.
PRINTED IN THE UNITED STATES OF AMERICA

1

Willy made the turn from the stairs toward the breakfast stool slowly, but too sharply. He hit his hip on the handrail post. "Ow," he said.

Nan didn't look up.

Willy clambered over his seat, dropped onto it hard and said, "Oooof!" It was spoken rather than genuinely exhaled. Nan recognized the difference.

"All right, all right," she replied, with the kind of patience that promises impatience to come. "I know you're tired. I know you're working hard. I know you have a deadline to meet. I know we need the money. I know you want special care and attention. I know it all. So you can give me a break from the full 'long-suffering' routine."

"I didn't say anything!" he protested, drawing his hands back. "All I said was 'Oooof,' a spontaneous ex-ywhatsit, often following or as a result of sudden pressure causing release of air through the throat and vocal cords."

Two slices of toast popped up in front of him.

"Toast!" he said.

"I heard you upstairs."

"What a wonderful wife!"

She slid a plate in front of him and handed him an envelope. There was already coffee in a cup next to the toaster. She sat down to eat a soft-boiled egg.

"Is this all the mail?"

Nan examined the ends of the egg, then sliced it lengthwise so it opened up like the halves of an avocado.

Willy shifted uneasily from buttock to buttock.

"I can't make Clarence write," Nan said without looking up.

"Agents are supposed to take care of you."

"He does."

"Especially when you're under pressure," Willy said. But he was conceding the point, as it was unarguable, and passing on to a curiosity about the contents of the envelope. "Who do we know in Terre Haute?" he asked, after making out the postmark.

1

"No one."

"You realize Terre Haute was the home of Theodore Dreiser."

"Sure," Nan said.

"And his brother Paul."

Nan took a breath and looked up at this. "And what did Paul Dreiser do for the world, Willy?"

"Not for the world. For Indiana." Willy was smiling and cheerful for the first time in the day. "He changed his name to Dresser and wrote 'On the Banks of the Wabash.'" Willy exaggerated a smile and held it for her, at her, to her. "It was made our state song in 1915."

Nan scooped some yolk onto a piece of bread with her knife and asked, "Words or music or both?"

"Damn," Willy said. "I don't know."

Nan savored her succulent white-and-yellow morsel while Willy buttered toast.

"There's no one in Terre Haute we'd be getting a bill from, is there?" he asked.

"It's not addressed to me."

"Shove the jam along, will you?"

Nan rose, picked up the jam and set it down next to his plate.

"I didn't mean for you to get up," he said.

"I was getting up anyway."

"Well, while you're up, is there another loaf of bread? Can I have the crust?"

"What's wrong with the one in front of you?" Next to the toaster, the crust and a last slice from a loaf of bread lay on a breadboard.

"Nothing. I feel like a matching pair of crusts, that's all."

"And you can't get it yourself?"

"But you were up. I said, 'while you're up.'"

"It means opening a new loaf."

While she got one and opened it, he said, "I had already figured that much out for myself."

"Here," she said, and dropped a second crust of bread next to the first.

Willy examined the letter for a return address.

"Are you working today?" Nan asked.

Willy looked up sharply, seeking the attack behind the question. Her face revealed none, so he said cautiously, "Of course. Why?"

"I just wanted to plan. You didn't yesterday and—"

"What makes you think I didn't work yesterday?"

"Well, in the morning."

"What about the morning?"

"I didn't hear any typing."

"Which proves?"

"All right," she said. "I just asked."

"And I just answered."

He spread some jam on the two pieces of toast he had already buttered. Cold, he thought, but he didn't say it. No, he thought; let's be fair. Cool.

Aloud he said, "I was working out a subplot."

She took the remaining slice of bread and jammed it without butter. Skillfully she asked, "Is it a fan letter?"

Willy opened the envelope and read the note it contained while eating one of the pieces of toast.

Finally he said, "Not exactly."

"It is only August," she said. "Still plenty of time for the annual unsolicited accolade."

"To be specific," Willy said, "the Terre Haute Writers' Circle has invited me to address its assembled throngs on Monday, May fourteenth."

"But that's months away!"

"At seven-thirty p.m. As they have seen my name in an index of Hoosier authors and some of their members are interested in crime fiction, would I be willing..."

Nan was amused.

"And, as I don't live in the environs of Terre Haute, they can offer me overnight hospitality if that would help make it possible to accept their invitation."

"How far is it? Fifty-five, sixty miles?"

"Seventy-one," Willy said. "Center to center, using limited-access roads wherever possible."

"Oh," Nan said.

"My brain is my only important asset."

"So you tell me."

"Ordinarily," he said, "I wouldn't consider staying overnight on a gig like that but..." He mused.

"Something to do with the banks of the Wabash?"

"It says 'hospitality.' Not just accommodation. It must be worth thinking about."

"Will you go?"

"I don't know. Anything on on May fourteenth?"

"Will you be finished with the current epic by then?"

"Very funny. Seriously, do I have anything else on?"

"Next year? How am I supposed to know?"

"You're the numerate one."

"I don't even have an appointments book for next year yet."

"So I'm free."

"Failing jail following bankruptcy action, I suppose you are. Unless you are planning to take one of your Indiana ramble months around then?"

"No," he said dismissively. "I'm going off after I send the book off, as usual."

Nan smiled.

"Very funny." He looked at the letter again. "I guess I'll write and ask for fifty bucks and gas. If they want me for that, they can have me."

She hesitated. "Are you serious?"

"About what?"

"Asking for fifty dollars?"

"They don't say anything about money. If they can't pay anything at all, usually they say so in the letter of approach."

"All of a sudden you're an experienced hand at this kind of thing, are you?"

"Well, writers' scuttlebutt. I've never been asked by Terre Haute, but there was Franklin College a couple of years ago."

"And scuttlebutt tells you the difference between accommodation and hospitality, too, does it?"

"Well, at my age I don't get many chances. I have to jump at crumbs."

"You have your memories."

"I guess so," Willy said. He ate his other piece of toast and then used a finger to pick up the crumbs from the plate.

"You going to eat those crusts?"

"I don't think so," he said.

Without comment she put them both into the wrapper with the new loaf and twisted the end shut.

"What's your schedule today?" he asked.

"I'm shopping this morning. And I'll be playing in the afternoon."

Willy watched Nan rinse the breakfast plates. "You're not going to the library, by any chance?"

"Hadn't planned to. Why?"

"I've decided to send Hank to England and I could use a book with maps and..." He waved his hands inarticulately. "That kind of thing."

She turned on him. "Hank, in England! Oh Willy, no!"

"Oh Willy, yes!"

"But why?"

"It's my subplot. I spent all yesterday morning working it out," he said pointedly.

"But Hank has trouble enough making himself understood to people from out of state. How's he going to handle England?"

"He'll Hank it out," Willy said with dignity.

"I suppose you know best, William."

"By this time, I should hope so."

"You..." she began hesitantly. "You remember we're going out to dinner."

He tried to remember.

"Lorraine. Larry and Lorraine Brinker."

"Ah yes," he said. "Of course. Larry's going to help me on antiques."

"Do you need help on antiques?"

"Well," he said, rocking back on the two rear legs of the stool, "the operation Hank finds is one in which European antiquities are smuggled into England, which is easy now that they've joined that Common Market, and then they're brought into the U.S. as extra parts of loads of English antiques. That's so the customs inspectors aren't looking for old Italian stuff and so on."

"Larry knows about that kind of thing?"

"He's mentioned antiques. It's worth a try. He can probably put me onto a book about it. I don't intend to make a big production of it, though. Most of what is going to happen in England is killing."

"You're not going to talk work all night, are you?"

"Well, I'm certainly not going to talk about the vicissitudes of the trailer business."

"Larry's not like that. He can be quite witty. I like listening to him talk."

"Guess that leaves me with Lorraine," Willy said.

"And good luck to you," Nan said.

"Who's your partner this afternoon? Playing with Howard,

or has he not managed to get time off again?"

She looked at her watch. "As a matter of fact, I am playing with Howard, yes."

Willy smiled.

Nan wiped down the breakfast counter.

Then Willy stood up. "I'm off," he said. "You're not making coffee before you go, by any chance?"

"If I do, I'll bring some up to you."

"Great."

"You're working two sessions?"

"Barring disaster."

"We're eating at eight and Lorraine doesn't want us to be late."

"O.K."

"I don't want to make a thing about it, but sometimes—"

"I understand," he said. "I understand. The muse will wrap up its second coming no later than seven-fifteen."

"I . . . All right."

"O.K., seven, then."

She smiled. "Seven."

"I'll be all right," he assured her. "I'll even keep awake."

"O.K."

"Right," he said. "Off to the wars."

2

CHAPTER XIX

"Look, babe," I told her. "I didn't invite you on this escapade. Your ever-loving hubby decided I needed a tour guide. I didn't put in a requisition for you."

"I am perfectly aware of that, Mr. Midwinter."

I pulled her to me by the ears so we were eyelash to eyelash. I was daring her to blink. I opened my lips but talked through the gaps in my teeth. "If you're going to come, you do it my way."

"But..."

"I call the tunes on my jobs. And if you or your husband don't like it I'll march you back to his goddamn restaurant, drop you in his art collection and let him find out for himself why his brother got shot."

"All right!" she said. I held on to her ears long enough for it to hurt. Her husband's money was so good I was willing to relax my rule about working alone, but it wasn't good enough to put up with someone giving me orders. I'm not the kind of guy that takes orders. That kind of guy is a waiter.

"So," I said, and I waved a finger in her face, "you tag along but you only give advice when you're asked for it. If I want some guiding, I'm not shy."

"All right, Mr. Midwinter," she said. The steely blue eyes melted like hot crayons.

"The name is Hank, Mrs. McKeand."

"All right, Hank," she said.

"And just because I tell you how it works, don't think you know where it's at. Don't make assumptions or half-assed offers. I'm not the kind of guy that has to jump at crumbs."

"I understand," she said. She lowered her face, then looked up at me through those gray eyelashes. I knew then I was going to have trouble with her. Bitches, molten in heat, harden to rock when they cool down.

But I'm not afraid of trouble.

*   *   *

I left her in the waiting room and went into Janine's office to touch her goodbye.

"Been listening on the intercom?"

"Of course," Janny said.

"What do you think?"

"I don't think you should take her with you, but since you've already decided to, I don't think you should turn your back on her."

Sometimes I think Janny knows me better than I know myself. "My stuff ready?"

"Of course."

I picked up an extra ball-point pen. I don't know much about England, but I was damned if I was going to be caught somewhere you couldn't get a ball-point pen. It's the little things you miss in underdeveloped countries.

"Hey, Janny, time for a goodbye quickie?"

She got those gold electric sparks in her big brown eyes, the way she does. "No," she said.

I fiddled with my ball-point.

"Not a goodbye quickie, Hank honey. An _au_ _revoir_ quickie."

"Just because you went to Radcliffe is no reason to talk foreign to me," I said.

"I hoped you'd ask," she said. "But do you have time to squeeze it in?"

"How long before I've got to be at the plane?"

She looked at her chronometer. "Thirty-three minutes before takeoff."

I ain't the first to say it, but there are occasions when actions speak more articulately than words.

*   *   *

When I left the office with Mrs. McKeand, we were four minutes behind schedule.

But The Doodah made up the time before the turn from Interstate 70 onto the Airport Expressway. The

Doodah is my four-wheeled flying machine. I have a
friend who looks after The Doodah, keeps her sweet
and at regular intervals gets bright little notions
about how to improve her accomplishments.

However much a private eye has to work alone,
there is no way you can get along without friends.
Loyal friends, who owe you and who you owe.

I checked The Doodah into the long-term parking
lot and let Mrs. McKeand carry her own baggage. On
this trip, she was mine.

*   *   *

I first noticed the guy when we were embarking.
He was a chubby pink man in a tweed overcoat.
People, normal people, just don't wear wool in
Indianapolis in August. It's not that he made me
nervous. He hadn't stirred since we took off. Or even
shaken. And as long as he didn't do anything but
sweat like a polar bear in the Sahara, it wasn't my
business. But I won't say I relaxed.

He made his move after we'd been flying for an
hour and a half. We were over some sticking-out bit of
Canada. The guy got out of his seat and walked back
toward the toilets. The overcoat was buttoned up to
the neck. It wasn't good.

3

Willy was lying sprawled on the couch in the living room with a saucer on his chest when Nan returned at 12:30. His eyes were closed. There was a red smudge at the corner of his mouth. She approached him quietly. She touched the red patch, tasted it.

"Blood from a cup wound," he said.

"Jam! You've had those two crusts—and smeared an inch thick, if I know you."

"Merely crusts of bread for a poor scribe," he said. He made his voice croak.

"Don't remind me of poverty," she said stiffly. "Not when I've just come from the supermarket."

With some seriousness, he said. "When I'm under stress, I have to do or eat what I feel like just so I don't add to my problems."

"And how did it go this morning?"

"Pretty well. I broke a bit early so I could start earlier this afternoon."

She nodded approval. He was reassuring her that he remembered their dinner thing. "Did you get your coffee?"

"Coffee?"

"Oh, for goodness' sake. I brought it up and left it outside your door. I knocked."

"God. I didn't hear."

"And you didn't notice it on your way down?"

He shook his head. The action caused the saucer to slip off his chest but he caught it before it reached the floor.

"I don't know why I bother," she said.

"One of the mysteries of life's threadbare tapestry."

"You going to rest this afternoon?"

"No. I want to go to the library to check out some maps of England. I need a town."

"You're really sending Hank over there then?"

"He's on the plane this very moment. In fact, he's in danger!"

"Oh yeah?" It was a non-inquisitive question.

"Just because there's a quarter of a book yet to go doesn't mean that he's automatically going to survive it."

"Why should this time be different?"

"Don't tempt me. I might kill him off."

"And have to work for a living?"

"So what's the matter with you?"

She shrugged, thought. "I'm sorry. I don't mean to knock Hank."

"I wouldn't mind giving him a knock from time to time myself," Willy said. "But what my public wants my publisher gets."

"That," she said, rather stiffly, "is the path you have chosen."

He rubbed his eyes.

"Will you have a lot of trouble making the deadline?"

"As long as I keep my mind churning and don't get to bed too late, I should be all right."

She nodded.

"Ah well. All part of life's rich confection." Suddenly he sat, then stood. "If I'm going to get back in time to work early to finish early, I've got to move."

"Willy?" A sense of worry in her voice.

"What now?"

"Are you maybe going to have time for a bit of a nap?"

"I don't know. I'll give it a stab, maybe."

"It's just that—"

He interrupted: "I know, I know. Last week's night out I fell asleep. But hell, I'm fifty-five. I'm supposed to do things like that in the face of utter boredom. It shows the increased maturity with which I deal with the problems I encounter as my life progresses."

"I'm not in the mood for that kind of garbage," Nan said, and walked out of the room.

Willy was old enough to remember the original library at Forty-second and Park. It wasn't one of the old Hoosier buildings he most regretted the loss of. Nor was the new building one he most welcomed. But librarians there treated him well, an honored patron, and he gave them copies of each new book as it came out.

"What can we do for you today, Mr. Werth?" asked the tall, gray Mrs. Rose.

"I'm looking for a town."

"All we have here is books," Mrs. Rose said. She smiled.

"Very nice," Willy said. Then he explained his need to pick out an English town and they consulted an atlas.

"Where do you want it?" Mrs. Rose asked.

"I don't really know."

"Well, large, small? Industrial, rural? North, south?"

Willy thought about Hank's plot needs while Mrs. Rose collected cash on two overdue books.

"O.K.," Willy said, on her return. "Small town in a sort of historical area. I'm setting up an antiques dodge, so it ought to be a part of England with historical connections."

"Everything over there has historical connections, Mr. Werth."

"I suppose so," Willy said. "I was there in the war and then again in 1958, but only around London." He frowned and looked at the United Kingdom map in the atlas. "God, look at the names they have for places," he said.

Mrs. Rose wasn't looking. "I've got a cousin whose husband's brother lives in a little town over there. Might that do?"

"What's it called?"

"Frome."

"Where is it?"

After a few minutes they found it in Somersetshire, south of Bath.

"Ah," Willy said, "now, Bath was an important town in Jane Austen's day."

"I suppose it was," Mrs. Rose said.

"Frome." Willy thought about it. "All roads lead to Frome."

"Do they? Oh! I see!"

"When in Frome, do as the Fromans. Yes, that will do fine. Just give me a couple of minutes with this book while I draw where it is and work out some of the distances to places."

Willy took notes for twenty minutes, then returned with the book to Mrs. Rose.

"I think," she said, "that I might be able to find out a few details about the place from my cousin. I'll call her."

"Well . . ." Willy was pleased. "If it wouldn't be too much trouble, a few details would be helpful. Just a bit, to make it seem real, as if I'd been there."

"I don't know whether they've actually visited," Mrs. Rose

said. "My cousin and her husband, I mean. But I will certainly
see what I can find out."

"I would appreciate that very much," Willy said truly.

Nan was out when Willy got home. Feeling tired, he went up
to bed to lie down. He was aware he'd said he would start his
second session early. So he knew he wouldn't be able to get
to sleep, but being horizontal for a few minutes felt good.

He worried then that there was something he had planned
to do that he had forgotten.

He fell asleep.

Later the telephone rang. And rang. Bleary, he fumbled for
it. "Hello."

There was a pause before the caller said, "William?"

"Yeah. Who's that—Charlie?"

"Sure. But I didn't recognize your voice. You sound different. Like . . . like you've got a clothesline around your neck
to see what being strangled feels like. Hey, ever think of that?"

"I was asleep."

"Oh, I am so so sorry," Charlie said pitilessly.

"Eat your heart out."

"You said you were coming down," Charlie said.

"Ahhh." Willy remembered what he'd forgotten.

"Don't." Charlie said. "Not now. I wanted to tell you that
I'm going home. If you haven't left yet, I won't be here when
you get here. Yeah?"

"O.K.," Willy said. "I'll take a nap instead."

"I've got to meet this guy about some termites."

"To tell the truth," Willy said, "I forgot I said I was
coming."

"You said you might, that's all," Charlie said.

"But I got this idea about sending Hank to England and I
went to the library to find out about it."

"I think it's somewhere across the ocean. Atlantic, Pacific,
one of those."

"What's this about termites? In your house?"

"You always were quick," Charlie said. "Yes, termites in
our house. I'm not really likely to have termites here at the
store." Charlie sold car parts. "Seeing as we're hundred percent
cinder blocks. Unless maybe they're cement-eating termites
from outer space. There's an idea for you."

"Just because Mitchell, Indiana, was the childhood home

of Gus Grissom doesn't mean all Hoosier writers have to do sci fi."

Charlie chuckled. "As a matter of fact, if you want to see something from outer space why don't you take a look through the exterminator ads in the Yellow Pages."

"Oh yeah?" Willy said.

Charlie hesitated. "If you want to, you can come over to the house a bit later."

Willy tried to remember why he couldn't come to the house later.

"It's just that Deb spent some time in England."

"Oh yeah?"

"Before I met her, part of her childhood. She might be able to help you with some detail."

"Hell, I remember. We're going out to dinner."

"Ah."

"Some people in Castleton."

"Suburb land. Anyone I know?"

"Guy called Larry Brinker. He sells trailers, but collects antiques. Hank is into a knot of antique hustles."

"A business dinner?"

"Well, not exactly."

"Nan doesn't know you're going to drain this guy's brain for tidbits for Hank to be a Philistine about, then?"

"One," Willy began measuredly, "must converse about something at a dinner. To keep awake, if nothing else."

"Whatever you say, brother."

"Say, if you could ask Deb about England for me, little things, I'd appreciate it."

"Why not ask her yourself?"

"I don't know if I'll have the time. I will if I do, but I'm under pressure to get this thing finished."

"Which is why you are going out to dinner."

"Don't hassle me, Charlie."

"Work hard, play hard."

"Don't ask her if you don't want to. The store's open tomorrow, isn't it?"

"If you mean will I be in tomorrow, I will," Charlie said. "Enjoy your time with your country-club friends."

"They got a daughter," Willy said, "who made a porno flick in New York."

"Have they, now?"

"It's just they're not your typical Castleton family."

"That's funny. Sounds to me like they are."

Willy lay back for a while and followed the brushstrokes of the paint on the ceiling. Then he rolled over to the telephone stand and pulled out the Yellow Pages.

There were seven pages of exterminator ads. A cutthroat business. "We kill termites, roaches, ants, fleas, spiders, moths, rats, mice, odors, ticks, weeds, flies and bedbugs."

Elsewhere they terminated "pigeons."

Clover mites, silverfish, snakes, mosquitoes, water bugs, squirrels, trees, bats and venomous arthropods, bees, wasps, hornets, yellow jackets.

"Help protect these": caption under a picture of two babies. "Don't talk to salesmen, talk to us." "No signs on our service trucks."

There were diagrams differentiating between flying ants and termites. There were lifetime guarantees, written reports, unionized workmen, service within one hour, twenty-four-hour seven-day service, free estimates, terms to fit your budget, two-way radio dispatching, discretion by a college graduate entomologist, assured integrity by former university instructor, bonds and insurance, reasonable rates and membership of national and state pest-control associations.

For all his improbable suggestions of things Willy could write about, Charlie had a fair sense for what would amuse. Willy wondered whether maybe he ought to go out to see Charlie and Deb to talk about England.

Dinner with the Brinkers. Oh yeah.

He went downstairs to the kitchen where he got a cold can of diet fizz from the refrigerator. He went to the back door and looked at the outdoor thermometer through the pane. It registered 89 degrees. It wasn't accurate, but it was good enough to tell him what he already knew.

He thought about walking around the garden. Instead he drank the fizz and went upstairs again.

4

I took the gold cigarette case from my inside jacket pocket.

The movement attracted Mrs. McKeand's attention. "I thought you didn't smoke," she said.

"I don't." I opened the case. "Look out the window."

"What?"

"Do what I tell you!"

She did it. It was just as well. I didn't have time to explain things to her. I didn't have much time at all.

But it only takes me ninety seconds to assemble the Louie Cigarette Case Special. It's a flat three-shot .22 caliber pistol.

I loaded it with three snub-nose shells out of my antihistamine bottle.

Louie is one of my friends. He makes me guns. I'd heard that this England was the kind of place where they are touchy about guys carrying guns. As a concession, I'd brought the Louie Cigarette Case instead of one of the other items he'd made for me. But a gun I had to have. This England was going to have to take me the way it found me. I'm one of those fellas who just doesn't feel dressed without a piece.

When Sweatbear came back from the john, I stood up and moved into the aisle behind him. He looked big and mean and bad, and he had his right hand under the coat now.

He passed the seat where he'd been sitting as if he'd never been taught how to sit. He was on his way to the pilot's cabin.

The only place I could take him out was the kitchen.

16

I caught up with him at the bulkhead seat,
pretended to trip and pushed him hard through the
curtains behind which lunch was being microwaved
into existence.

We hit a redhead on the rump as we went down.

She squealed, but wasn't caught underneath. I
groped to pin the guy's hand to his stomach. I found
something; it was a whopper.

But a little one in the right place does the job. I
stuck the Cigarette Case Special in his mouth. I took a
few teeth along in the process.

The redhead was on her feet. I said to her, "Pull the
curtain closed!"

She closed it.

To my friend I said, "If you give me so much as one
wiggle, I'll pull the trigger and you'll never play the
piano again."

I could feel the guy tensing.

I cocked the gun.

I could feel him relax. People say I have a way with
words.

"Let go of your gun," I said.

He thought about it for a minute.

I pushed the Special farther into his mouth, up to
my knuckles.

He let go. I grabbed it, and we rolled once over
lightly as I pulled it out. It was a Colt M1911, the .45.
I unloaded it and then tapped my friend on the head
with the barrel. I never hit people on the head with
the butt. I hate looking up the wrong end of a gun.

*　　*　　*

Mrs. McKeand's face could have lost itself in a
gallon of vanilla ice cream.

"What happened?" she hissed at me urgently.

"Lunch is going to be a little late," I said. I
dismantled my tiny gun and put it back behind the
cigarettes.

She was furious as she watched. She screamed at
me with her mind. When I put the case away and
snapped the childproof top back on the antihistamine

bottle, she asked again, "What happened, you bastard. Tell me."

"I've just been making friends with the good-looking stewardess—you know, the redhead."

I would have been happy to tell her all about it. But she didn't say "please."

*   *   *

We waited till the plane cleared before we moved to disembark ourselves. The stewardess had the Captain waiting. He was a stocky little guy with a hatchet face, ugly enough to be a real ladies' man. He gave Mrs. McKeand a good looking-over.

But it was my hand he shook. "Stewardess Smith has told me how effectively you handled our unwelcome passenger, Mr. Midwinter."

"Do you know who he is or where he would have taken us?" I asked.

"No."

"Why not stick his head in your microwave oven for a while?" I suggested. "I'm sure given the right preparation, he'd cook up a story for you."

"We'll leave that to the authorities, shall we," the Captain said. "I alerted Scotland Yard by radio while we were in the air and they have taken him off already."

"Scotland Yard?" I said. "What's this got to do with Scotland?"

I was pulling his leg but he didn't feel the tug.

"No, you see—" he began.

"Don't explain," I said, "we gotta go. Glad I was able to help." I nodded Mrs. McKeand to the hatch.

"Well, thank you again," the Captain said.

"I'd like to thank you, too," the redhead said. She shook my hand. There was a piece of paper in our joint grip. I took it with me. "I hope you have a pleasant stay in England," she said.

In the line waiting to show our passports, I had a look at the note. "My name is Donna. I have stopovers tomorrow, the 16th and the 19th." It gave her phone number.

There are worse ways of entering a new country.

CHAPTER XX

At the airport ((Find out Name of Airport)), Mrs.
McKeand gave me a hard time because the first thing
I did was rent a car. She wanted to go to a hotel.

"I'm tired," she said.

"Go to sleep then."

"But—!"

"I'm a working man. I give value for money. It's
morning here. So I'm on my way to Frome."

"But you've got to sleep sometime." She was
whining now.

"When I'm in Frome, I'll sleep like the Fromans."

"But I'm tired," she said again.

I left her, following directions to the place I could
pick up my car. I found it, a kind of Ford, only I'd
never seen one so small. After I put my suitcase in
the back seat, I also found Mrs. McKeand, behind me.

"You don't have to walk so fucking fast," she said.

There's not much you can say to that.

*   *   *

Frome was west of ((Airport)) about ninety miles.
Sixty-five of them were on a freeway, but the rest was
across country. I was disappointed. Not many roads
lead to Frome.

For sixty miles the boss's wife dozed and was quiet.
I was grateful, but didn't wake her up to tell her so.
Then she woke up and out of the blue asked me a
question.

"Have you ever killed a man?"

"You mean with my bare hands or shot one or
what?"

"With your bare hands!" she said, as if she had
never heard that hands can be lethal.

"The only time with hands," I said, "was when I
choked a lady who talked too much."

It did the trick for five miles, but for some reason
turning off the freeway brought her mind back to
killing.

"And with a gun?"

"A few," I said. There was a space to pull over just

after we made the turn. I pulled up into it and turned to face her.

"I've also killed with a knife and a rope. But in each case it was a matter of protecting lives, sometimes my own. The only time I have killed a man without benefit of a weapon was by accident."

"How do you kill someone by accident without a—"

"It was in a fight. A guy was trying to strangle me and we were jockeying around because I was against the idea. I was able to bring my knee up hard in his balls."

After a moment, "That killed him?"

"It can take people that way. It happened to be a real good shot."

She seemed to think. "What a terrible way to go," she said.

You wouldn't catch me disagreeing, except when that's fatal, death is instantaneous.

But I had other things on my mind.

"Why," I asked her, "all the questions about killing people?" It was a serious question and I put it forcefully. "I want to know what you are trying to tell me."

"I'm not trying to tell you anything," she said. "I was just asking."

"I don't believe you. You're asking because you want to know whether I am up to killing people if I have to. Right?"

"I was only asking," her voice said, but her eyes were smug.

"And if you're thinking about that, then you're thinking about someone I'm going to run into I may have to kill. I think I ought to know about that."

"There's nothing," she said. "It was just talk."

It was not the kind of subject for ordinary small talk. But I didn't have the time or energy to torture the answers to my questions out of her.

Rented cars don't come complete with microwave ovens.

Pity. Maybe if they had, if she'd told me why she asked about killing people, she might have stayed alive herself.

5

Nan was in the kitchen. She was making a sandwich.

Willy stood in the doorway. "I thought we were going out to eat."

"We are."

"I'm not late down, am I? They haven't canceled, have they? God, I'm whacked."

"Oh, you're not tired, are you!"

"I've been working hard, that's all. Work-tired, not tired-tired. I'll go sit down for a while, unwind." He went to the living room and lay down on the couch.

Nan followed. "I was hungry," she said.

"But peanut butter! When you're going to eat again in a couple of hours!"

"An hour and forty minutes," she said.

Willy still felt tired as they set out for Castleton, but instead of sitting silent he talked about Hank. "His client's wife is a nag, but she's about to meet a terrible end."

"Oh yes?"

"She has a grisly death coming, but it's her own fault. She talks when Hank wants her to be quiet."

"Vengeance is swift and just."

After being quiet for a minute, Willy said, "It's not Hank that's killing her, you know."

"No, I didn't think so."

"O.K."

"Are you still sending him to England?"

"He's already there. He's on his way to a place called Frome."

"Never heard of it."

"Neither had I, but I've got a librarian working on it for me. Though they all must look a lot like one another, these little towns. I imagine them like the old parts of London we saw. Cobbled streets and all that."

"But that was 1958."

"These old countries don't change much, do they?"

· "If they did, Hank probably wouldn't notice the difference," she said.

"Don't knock Hank. I can knock Hank, but don't you knock Hank. You know," Willy said irritably, "I get a bit tired of you acting like I am an insensitive boor just because my detective is. I can understand why other people get Hank and me confused, but I expect more discrimination from you."

"Well, you're not exactly an answer to Indiana's cultural deprivation, are you?"

"I suppose we're off and running on the 'I expected you to take me away from corncob pipes' bit. Well, I never promised you I was going to write about Grecian urns."

Nan was silent.

"Nothing to say?"

"Not really, but I'm not the one who is tired and irritable."

"I am like hell."

Nan shrugged.

"I know, I know," Willy said. "Hank is a collection of all my worst characteristics."

"Not all of them," Nan said. "Hank doesn't go to sleep at dinner parties."

"I'm not going to sleep, all right! Give it a goddamn rest, will you?"

At a stoplight in the Castleton suburb of Indianapolis, Willy didn't start again when the light changed.

"It's green," Nan said.

"I know." He said it softly.

She looked behind them.

"It's clear," Willy said before she spoke. "I'm not inconveniencing anyone by my little aberration."

She looked at him and was slightly puzzled.

Willy sighed. "And the fact that I check to make sure it's clear before I allow myself to aberrate is a measure of why I write about Hank instead of about . . . nightingales."

"Have you ever seen a nightingale?"

Willy didn't say anything.

"Or heard one?"

"I get poetic feelings and inspirations. More than most people. Maybe more than most writers. I just don't do anything about them."

The light changed to yellow.

"You call sitting through a green light poetic?"

"Yes."

Nan turned away. Willy put a palm to his forehead.

"How many lights are you going to sit through?"

He answered the real question. "I didn't intend to annoy you. That wasn't the intention."

A motorcycle pulled up behind them. When the light changed to green again, Willy started promptly, but the motorcyclist roared past them.

As Willy made the turn off the Fort Wayne Road, he said, "They came to our place the end of June, didn't they?"

"Yes."

"Has anything happened since then that I should know about?"

"Happened?"

"Come on, don't give me a hard time. Happened. To them. Is there anything I should remember that I'm likely to forget?"

Relenting, Nan said, "Not really. Only that movie, but you won't have forgotten that."

"Oh yeah," Willy said. "I remember now. The daughter, wasn't it? How many kids do they have?"

"Only the one."

The Brinker house was one of a number spread along a road rising up a hill. As they drove up to it, Willy and Nan saw two cars on the roadside.

They realized at the same time that one was a marked police car; wondered silently at the same time whether it could be anything to do with the Brinkers; when closer, they tried at the same time to think whether it could possibly not be something to do with the Brinkers.

Willy hesitated before turning into the driveway.

"What do you think that's all about?" he asked.

"Should we go in?" Nan asked.

Willy pulled into the driveway. "What else can we do? Hell, it's probably nothing. What can it be?"

Cement steps wound upward to the front door. Nan took Willy's arm.

The door opened before they rang the bell. A heavyset man of about forty-five faced them. He told them to come in with such a sense of authority that they entered the house without questioning or speaking. Neither Willy nor Nan had ever seen the man before.

"Now," the stranger said, "who might you be?"

"William and Nancy Werth," Willy said.

"What are you doing here?"

"We were invited for dinner," Nan said.

The man turned from them toward the rear of the entrance hall. There a younger man in police uniform stepped out. "They say they were asked for dinner. Check with the wife." The man in uniform disappeared.

"Where do you live?"

Willy gave their address. Then asked, "What's going on?"

"Are you friends of the Brinkers?"

"Yes."

"How long have you known them?"

"About two or three years."

"I've known Lorraine Brinker longer than that," Nan said. "But we've only seen each other as families about that long."

"Now," Willy began again, "we've helped—"

From the back of the house a frantic voice was heard, and a moment later Lorraine Brinker pushed past the uniformed man into the hall.

"It's Larry!" she said. She ran into Nan's open arms.

"Is he dead?" Willy asked without thinking.

"Oh God! He can't be!" Lorraine began to cry.

The heavyset man spoke gently to Nan. "Take her back to the kitchen, will you, Mrs. Werth? Her husband is missing, that's all. He'll probably walk in in an hour or two, but we've come out to make sure we don't get caught by surprise. There is certainly no reason to suspect foul play at this juncture." The man looked severely at Willy.

Nan led Lorraine down the hall and back into the room from which she had come.

When they were out of sight, the heavyset man said to Willy, "Now, Mr. Werth, do you have any reason to think that Mr. Brinker is dead?"

"What? No!" Willy said. "It...it was just the first thing that came to my mind."

"Do you always say the first thing that comes into your mind?"

All Willy could think to reply was "No."

"If this business drags out and Mr. Brinker should fail to

come home tonight, please try to think about what effect loose speculation might have on Mrs. Brinker's frame of mind. Don't say anything disturbing in her presence. If, for instance, we are in a kidnapping situation, we want her as calm as we can get her."

Willy nodded. He wondered if he and Nan were going to be asked to stay around all evening.

"If it comes to a moment when she has to make a decision," the man continued, "it would be in everybody's interest that she be as rational as possible."

"I understand," Willy said, though he didn't quite. "How long has Larry been missing?"

"I would appreciate it," the man said, "if you would answer a few questions for me. It might help."

Willy nodded.

"How well would you say you know Mr. Brinker?"

"Fairly well. Well, not that well."

"When did you see him last?"

"They came to dinner at our place at the end of June."

"You exchanged meals about every six weeks then?"

"More or less."

"Did you see Mr. Brinker at other times?"

"Parties sometimes. As my wife said, she knew Lorraine before. Through playing bridge. We didn't meet as couples until—"

"The last two or three years," the man interrupted. "Yes, you said."

"I did once play squash with Larry. But he was out of my class. I just wasn't enough opposition for him for us to play again. I don't really play very often and—"

"What I am getting at," the heavyset men said, "is whether you have any idea of a reason Mr. Brinker might have had to leave home suddenly."

"Oh," Willy said.

"Did you have any feeling that he might be dissatisfied with his life in some way?"

"You mean to kill himself?" The idea had never crossed Willy's mind. "Good heavens, is that what you think?"

"I'm asking what you think, Mr. Werth. Why, for instance, you think of suicide in relation to Mr. Brinker rather than, say, his having run off with a woman friend? Or a man friend, or because of business debts?"

The man waited for Willy to answer, but Willy didn't quite

know what he had been asked. He was feeling shaky now from
having been thrust unexpectedly into a complex and unfamiliar
situation.

"Well," the man said, "why did you ask whether he had
killed himself?"

"I don't know," Willy said.

"Was he a gambler, an excessive drinker? Did he have any
domestic problems that you know of?"

"Not that I know of."

"Do you know anything which might help us understand
how Mr. Brinker comes to be missing without explanation for
more than a day?"

"I didn't know him . . . don't know him terribly well," Willy
said. "But I must say it doesn't sound like Larry Brinker at
all."

The man took it as a feeble answer. "All right, Mr. Werth.
Go on into the living room, will you, and sit down. Until your
wife is ready to leave."

Willy sat as directed.

He had only a few minutes to wonder whether he should
be doing something else when Nan came.

Willy stood up. "How is she?"

"They have a policewoman there to look after her. They say
we should go."

"There's nothing we can do?"

"Like what?"

"I don't know. We could sort of stand by, in case there was
something."

"Come on," Nan said. "We're best out of their way."

They walked back to the hall and the heavyset policeman.
He opened the door for them and didn't speak as they left.
Willy wanted to offer to help, but the man did not inspire
conversation.

"You were right," Willy said as they closed themselves into
the privacy of their car. "We're best out of the way."

"Lorraine is in a terrible state," Nan said.

"What's happened? Did you get more of the story?"

"Larry didn't come home last night. He said he was staying
late to work."

"On a Sunday night?"

"He had paperwork to catch up on. But he didn't come
home and he didn't call, either."

"Hmm."

"So he's been gone for twenty-six or twenty-seven hours without letting her know what's happening."

"When did she call the police?"

"In the middle of the night. Two or three times before they came out finally. The policewoman said they don't usually count someone as missing until they've been gone longer than that."

"That's right," Willy said.

"But Lorraine has been up all night. Calling hospitals, calling wherever she could think. Oh, and she apologized for not having warned us about dinner. She said it completely slipped her mind."

"It is hard to think of an explanation," Willy said. "One that isn't bad."

"Lorraine is half crazy. Boo is coming in. I don't know whether anyone else is."

"Boo?"

"Barbara. The daughter."

"Do you want to stay with Lorraine tonight, Nan? If she's got nobody."

"I offered. But she decided no."

"What will happen," Willy said, "is that he will just walk in the front door in a couple of hours."

Nan was silent.

"Maybe amnesia or something. It has to happen in real life occasionally for it to be used so often in fiction."

"They think he's been kidnapped," Nan said.

"He isn't that rich, is he?" Willy was surprised.

"Maybe it's by mistake," Nan said. "Who knows? Can we go?"

"The cop asked me if Larry had a girl friend he might have run off with."

"A girl friend?"

"Or a boyfriend. Or whether there was some other reason I knew why Larry would take off."

"What did you say?"

"I said I didn't know of any reason. What else could I say? I don't know of any."

Nan sat, again quiet. Then she said, "Please let's go home. Come on, let's get away from here."

Willy put his hand lightly on her shoulder. She put her

hands to her eyes. He started the car and backed out of the driveway slowly.

When they were back in the house, Willy asked, "What shall we do about food? Shall I make something?"

"I don't feel like eating. Make something for yourself. I'm a bit upset."

They walked through to the living room and sat down on the couch.

"You know," Willy said, "I should have asked a lot of things."

"What do you mean?"

"That guy in the hall."

"The policeman?"

"I should have asked to see his credentials."

"Oh Willy, don't be stupid."

"It's the kind of thing everybody advises you to do. Ask for ID, record the number. I don't even know his rank. Or his name, for that matter."

"Sergeant Hearns," Nan said. "They talked about him in the kitchen. Besides, there were police cars out front."

"I'm not saying he wasn't a real policeman. But there it was, just about the only time in my life I've ever been confronted by a real police situation and all I did was kowtow and sit when I was told to. I should have asked more questions myself. I should have been more aggressive, that's all I'm saying."

"What good would it have done?"

"Well, I'm supposed to know a bit about these things," Willy said.

Nan didn't say anything.

"What are you going to do, call Lorraine later or wait till tomorrow?"

"They said I shouldn't call. They're waiting for a phone call and they don't want people tying up the line."

"Ah," Willy said.

"Lorraine said she'd let us know when there was something to let us know. Oh Willy, it was so sad. She said she'd call, unless we heard about it on the TV first."

"God," Willy said. "Brings it home to you, doesn't it?"

6

We got to Frome about half past eleven. We made
good time. It looked just like I expected an English
town to look. ((fill in descriptive material when it
comes in))

Cute little houses, cute little cars, cute little people.

"Seems like a good place for an antiques racket," I
said to Mrs. McKeand. "Even the new stuff looks old."

"Are you really the Philistine you pretend to be, Mr.
Midwinter?"

"Yes," I said. I wouldn't lie to a client's wife. With
one, maybe, but not to one.

We checked into the hotel in the middle of town.
Separate rooms. Then ate in the hotel dining room. I
had steak. That is to say, I ordered a steak. What came
was the right shape, but so thin it looked like a slice
of bloody cardboard. I ordered three more, and ate the
stack, flapjack-style.

After it was over, I said, "Right, time for bed."

She brought her head up sharply, and her eyes
came alive.

I smiled my winning toothy country-boy grin.
"Shucks, ma'am, I just reckoned you must be powerful
tired by now."

She hesitated. "Look, Mr. Midwinter..."

"Even m'enemies call me Hank, ma'am."

She hesitated, then broke. "If you'll call me Stella,"
she said.

"Shucks, Mrs. McKeand, what with you bein'
m'client's wife it wouldn't hardly be fittin' for me to
do that." I kept smiling.

"Are you a bastard or just an asshole? Or are you
going to give me crap about not mixing business with
pleasure?"

"Ain't hardly no point in mixing business with
business."

29

"Please," she said. "Don't play with me."

I stopped smiling and nodded. "All right, Mrs. McKeand. But it's still time you had a nap."

"What about you?"

"I want to do some scouting round before the sun goes down."

"What happens then?"

"Then we both go visiting those people who were involved with your husband's brother's business. We let them know we're here and then, I think, they'll come to us."

"Is it wise to let them come to us?"

I shrugged. "We don't have much choice, do we?"

She didn't say anything.

I paid the bill and we went to her room and I found she could do things with her mouth besides nag.

Later I tucked her in and went out for a walk. It was ten past two on ((Hell, I need that Frome material here. Better phone the library and see if I can track down Auntie or whoever it was, rather than waiting for them to call me))

7

There was a space in front of the store, so Willy didn't bother to pull into the parking lot.

Behind the counter a woman in green overalls was bent over an open parts catalog. "Hang on a sec, will you?" she asked without looking up. Rather than walking through, Willy waited. He was curious.

When the woman, who was in her late twenties, finished with the book, Willy said, "You're new, aren't you?"

"About three weeks," she said.

"I'm Charlie's brother. Is he around?"

"He's in the yard, I think. You're the writer, aren't you?"

"Yup."

"I haven't read any of your books."

"Neither have I."

"Oh."

"I know my way, thanks," Willy said.

Charlie left the yard and came into the office so he and Willy could talk.

"Since when did you start hiring women to sell car parts?"

"Since the best applicant for the job turned out to be a woman."

"Yeah?" Willy turned to the wall behind which the parts counter was.

"She was with the Hell's Angels for fifteen years and kept her ears and eyes open in the process."

Willy turned back to his brother. "Really?"

Charlie smiled. "There's an angle for you. Interesting character."

"Pity I don't believe a word of it," Willy said.

"Know cars."

"Mmm."

"Did you ask her for anything?"

"No."

31

"On your way out, ask her for a double swing-weight interlock for a fifty-eight Thunderbird. See how long it takes her."

"A what? Say it again," Willy said, getting his notebook out.

"She'll know, even if you don't, that there is no such thing."

"Oh. Funny fellow today, eh?"

"Bit early for you to be out and about, isn't it?"

"Yeah, but I got stuck needing some information. So I had to break work only to get it. And since I was nearby, I thought I'd stop and catch the latest in the termite saga."

"What information?"

"About a little town in England. Called Frome. Well, apparently they pronounce it Froom, but I'm not going to bother with that."

"You don't mean a big town in Italy by any chance?"

"No, Charles. My librarian put me on to a cousin who visits there. I've just been to see her and she gave me all kinds of good stuff. Pictures, maps . . ."

"Yer ye olde genyuwine authentical details, huh?"

"That's it. Just what I needed. Hank went over for what was going to be just a quick in and out but—"

"A quick in and out. Oh boy, William. What a way with words."

"But," Willy continued, "I may keep him there a little bit longer."

Charlie smiled, and not without interest. Then he said, "Deb knows quite a bit about England."

Willy mused momentarily. "Nan and I went over in fifty-eight. To London. But that was to promote the movie they made out of *Hayride Horror*."

With a wry smile Charlie said, "I forgot about that."

"Just as well. But it bought the house."

"And at least you don't have termites."

"Is it serious?"

"Bad enough. But the place isn't going to fall down." Charlie leaned back and shrugged. Then, puzzled, he asked, "What the hell is Hank doing in England? He's never been out of Hoosierland before, has he?"

"Chicago and Cincinnati."

"England, huh? A small step for mankind, but a giant step for Henry Midwinter."

"Yeah."

"He's not going to have to go without his Wheaties for breakfast, is he?"

"They gotta have Wheaties there, don't they?" Willy whined on Hank's behalf. "Aw jees."

"They say," Charlie said, "that England is a land of opportunity just like America."

"Do they?" Willy said. Alerted by tone of voice for a set piece.

"Well, not quite the same," Charlie said. "Here every boy can grow up to be President, but over there every boy can grow up to be a queen."

"Oh."

"Feel free to quote me."

"I'll make a note. But they do have faggots over there."

"They have faggots everywhere."

"No, something called faggots. A food. The lady was telling me about them."

"Faggots from Frome?"

"They're a kind of meatball made by the butchers out of the leftovers they have. You bake them and have them with gravy."

"And chips? Everything with chips."

"But of course!"

Charlie pursed his lips and said, "You know, Deb spent part of her childhood in England."

"I think you said."

"Yup. Part of her rainbow background."

"Mmm."

They were quiet for a moment.

"How," Charlie asked, "was dinner with your fancy friends?"

"It didn't take place."

"What you mean?"

"Place was crawling with cops. Larry—that's the husband—hadn't been home for twenty-four hours."

"There's a lot of it about," Charlie said. "What happened?"

"They don't know."

"Doesn't sound good."

"I suppose not. Aw, hell, he'll probably walk in or something."

"Maybe," Charlie said.

"I've got to go," Willy said, and rose. "I just stopped in to say hello."

"Hello," Charlie said.

Getting into his car outside Charlie's, Willy felt an urge to head into the city to the Police Department to track down Sergeant Hearns and find out the current status of the Larry Brinker case. He thought about it, but dismissed the urge as atavistic, born out of an old reflex to delay work when the pressure to work was greatest.

He overcame himself and went home.

8

I paid the bill and we went to her room. I found she could do things with her mouth besides nag.

After I tucked my client's wife into bed for her nap, I went out for a walk. The post office clock read ten past two. On the Market Place Information Board I found a map that showed how to get to the address I had for George McKeand's business. I had to walk up an old street with a sluice of water running down the middle. Funny way to build a street. It was called Cheap Street but they could have been had for false advertising.

The place I was going to was called Auntie's Antiques. It was not a large storefront, though the window was spiked with lots of old-looking stuff. You'd have thought it was a business. But it was the base for the McKeand brothers' operation. On the door it said "Open." I didn't go in. I walked on up the street to Church Steps, past St. John's Church and the length of Gentle Street. That's where the sex shop was.

In the sex shop I asked directions to the police station. All sex shops can give directions to the nearest police station.

CHAPTER XXI

"Look, Constable, ma Cousin Georgie got hisself killed here! It's only natcheral as how I'd wanna stop an' ask what y'all are doin' about it, seein' as how I was comin' to this country on a li'l vacation anyhows." If I was doing my best to be a good old country boy, he was certainly the archetypal British copper, with the blue suit, big blue hat and everything.

"Jolly decent of you to take an interest, of course."

"It's more than a interest. He was fambly! We can't

35

hardly believe as how he's dead and gone. An' in a quiet, peaceable lovin' country like this here England! It jes don't seem right. Have you caught the low-down killer yet?"

"No sir, we haven't."

"Well, when y'all gonna get him?"

"I can't actually say."

"Well, hell, what can you say? Do y'all know who it was that done it?"

"Well sir, we feel strongly that George McKeand was murdered by someone who knew him well. As he was not considered a very social person, we feel there is good reason to interview his associate in business. Unfortunately the associate, one Brock Hallett, has not been seen in Frome since the crime was committed nineteen days ago."

"But I jes' came through the town an' their ole shop had a open sign on it."

"Business is being maintained by the shop assistant, Miss Mayhew, with our approval on the chance of Mr. Hallett making a reappearance. But we don't know Hallett's whereabouts, and our experience with Americans is that they can be just about anywhere. So I fear I am unable to hold out much hope for an early resolution of the case."

"You reckon he's gonna get away, huh?"

"I wouldn't want to say that, sir."

"But you don't know where to look for him."

"We do find foreign suspects somewhat unpredictable, yes."

"Can y'all tell me this—how exactly was Cousin Georgie killed?"

"He was shot, sir. Eight times with a medium-caliber handgun. A Walther PPK, to be precise."

"Eight .32 caliber slugs. Emptied the thing into him. Wow."

"It was not an attractive sight, sir, I can assure you."

"No robbery or nothin'?"

"We feel the motives were personal and the killer was not a stranger."

"O.K.," I said. "I sure do hope you catch that guy.

The whole fambly's with you guys, so hang in there,
y'hear?"

"We'll do our very best, sir. I assure you."

I walked out of the place wondering whether their
best was going to be good enough.

I <u>knew</u> it wasn't going to be fast enough.

*   *   *

I made my way quickly down the hill into town
and back to Auntie's Antiques. This time the sign on
the door said "Closed." I tried the handle. The door
was locked. But the newly made doorframe didn't look
all that solid, so I pushed and it gave way.

In the middle of tables of green brass and dusty
china I shouted, "Where the hell are you?"

I heard a rush of activity above me. Footsteps fairly
flying down the stairs. From the back of the store a
dramatic-looking woman emerged: thin intelligent,
sophisticated, hair glittering with gold-and-auburn
highlights. She didn't look like Auntie. I suspected
that she was not just a shop assistant. Impulsively I
backed my hunch.

"You've seen Brock Hallett today," I said.

"He...he was upset. He'd seen a man in town, who
just came here—"

"Where is he now?"

"I don't know. I don't know." Tears came to her
eyes. She groped on her person for a concealed
handkerchief.

"What's your name, child?" I asked.

"Henna Mayhew." She wiped her eyes and took a
breath as if she had to snatch it. "It means he's going
to leave. I knew it, when he said about the man."

"He isn't the kind of person a girl should get
herself caught on, Henna."

"We don't choose, do we?" Flame leapt from her
eyes.

"A murderer?"

"He told me all about that! It was an accident!"

I didn't pursue the subject. Instead I asked, "What
is it that makes you so involved with him?"

"I think, in the end, it's because he's so tactile."
I left her to her memories.

*   *   *

But outside the store, on the sidewalk, I
experienced another kind of tactile. I was tapped upon
the shoulder.

I turned to face a woman with long brown hair
who was wearing a peppermint-stripe suit.
"Midwinter?"

"I hope we can get it together before then," I said.

9

After two minutes of finding flower shapes in the abstract pattern of his office wallpaper, Willy realized that he wasn't working. He leaned back from his typewriter and swiveled in his chair. A break in concentration. He then felt himself moved by an impulse. This time he got up, went to the car and drove to town.

Police headquarters in Indianapolis is on the corner of Alabama and Market Streets, occupying about half of the faceless complex that is the City-County Building. The entrance is on Alabama, across from the parking lot, adjoining the Market Square Arena.

Just inside the door, on the right, Willy found a reception counter. A uniformed officer came to him from behind a desk. "Can I help you?"

"I truly do hope so," Willy drawled. "I got me a member of my fambly, a cousin, he is what was reported missin' a couple days ago and I surely would like to know how things stand about him. Whether he has yet been found, that kind of thing?"

"Did you report him missing, sir?"

"No, no. I'm just here as a kind of interested party from the fambly, you know. No, his wife, she reported him missin'."

The police officer looked at Willy and frowned. "May I have your name, please?"

"The name of the man what's missin'," Willy said, "is Mr. Larry Brinker and he lives in Castleton. It's a Mr. Sergeant Hearns that is in charge of the case."

"You want to see Sergeant Hearns, is that it?"

"No," Willy said, "I'm just a tryin' to find out the current state of affairs with the missin' situation of Mr. Larry Brinker."

"Well, what does Mrs. Brinker say?"

"Well, I didn't want to bother Lorraine with what might seem like idle curiosity," Willy said.

"You'd rather bother us with idle curiosity?" The policeman was getting angry.

"I'm not meaning to bother you. That is not my purpose. But—"

"Go on, go away! Get out! Get out!"

As he left, Willy heard the man mutter, "Sheee-it!"

Nan was in the kitchen when he got back.

"I've just made a colossal fool of myself," he announced as he walked in.

"I've just made a strawberry shortcake," Nan said. "I got some late strawberries cheap and I just couldn't resist."

"Don't you care that your husband has just made a colossal fool of himself?"

Nan looked at him and chuckled. "I know you find it annoying, but I think you are so funny when you take things so seriously."

For a moment Willy raged. But then sniffed. "Oh, well."

"What was it this time, hon?"

"This time? This time? What is it, I make a fool of myself all the time, every day?"

"No. Of course not. I'm sorry." She turned away, stifling a smile.

"All right."

"Come through and tell me," she said.

They walked through to the living room and sat on the couch.

Willy explained how he had had a shot at trying to extract information from the police by passing himself off as a relative of the Brinkers. "It seemed like a good idea at the time."

"Was there something special you were trying to find out?"

"Not really."

"It seems a strange thing to do," she said, the mildest wording for her feelings she could muster.

He couldn't quite bring himself to tell her that he had gone to it straight from having Hank do the same kind of thing, successfully. "The Impulse Imperative," he said, and sighed.

"Poor William. Has it been a hard day?"

"I guess so," he said.

"You're on schedule, aren't you?"

"Nearly. I didn't expect to send Hank to England. And, being a late decision, I wasn't quite ready with background information and all that."

"You can get it."

"I got most of it today. Saw my librarian's cousin. Got quite a bit of good stuff."

"Well, it'll be all right."

They sat silently for a moment. Then Willy said, "It's part of my professional responsibility to act on my impulses. It's how I explore my psyche to develop the depth of my characters."

"Save it for the Terre Haute Writers' Circle," Nan said.

"It's just that I have this feeling, I guess, that I should do something."

"About what?"

"About Larry Brinker."

"Do something? What?"

"I don't know."

"I think you'll feel better when you've done a bit more work," she said.

10

"Hank Midwinter?"

She had piercing blue eyes and a penetrating body. I nodded.

"If you want information about George McKeand, follow me."

She turned her back on me and walked away. In a stride I had her by the shoulders. I spun her to face me.

If I weren't a suspicious character, governed by instincts of self-preservation, the projecting knuckles would have left me clutching my solar plexus and gasping for air.

I caught the blow in my hand.

"All right," I said. "You're trained. What's this all about?"

"You've had my message," she snapped. "Take it or leave it."

The center of a foreign town is a poor location to intimidate information out of someone. "I don't have my car with me," I said.

"Get it. I'll be parked in front of your hotel in seven minutes. I will leave the front of your hotel in eight minutes. And that will be that."

"Except I don't know which one your car is."

She looked at me and smiled. "It will be the one with me in it."

*   *   *

Seven and a half minutes later, in front of the hotel, I spotted her in a red car so little it was hard to tell whether it was standing or sitting down. I pulled up behind it and saw it was called a Mini. Probably because you could put a miniskirt around it and not know it was there.

But the lady was. In a puff of blue smoke, she pulled away and led me into the country.

I hadn't slept.

That's my excuse for it taking nearly half an hour of wandering through villages of the like of Mells, Nunney and Chantry before I realized I was being led by the nose to nowhere. Her mistake was to take me twice through Vobster.

Maybe she thought that I wouldn't be paying attention to the name. But coming from a state with towns like Ladoga, Bear Branch, Montmorenci and Philomath, I stay alert to names of places. Alert, that's another Indiana town.

I followed her through a turn to something called Shepton Mallet and then jammed her little car up against the bank of the first open stetch of country lane that we hit.

She got out angry. "What the hell did you do that for!"

I took hold of the lapels of her peppermint suit. "You're leading me round and round the blueberry bush."

"Don't be stupid," she said.

I lifted her so high that her seams began to rip. It brought her close. She smelled good. "You stink," I said. "You've got sixty seconds to tell me what, if anything, you know about George McKeand."

"I know it looks bad," she said after the first five. "But I got lost."

"You've got fifty-one left."

I'm a fearsome sight when I'm roused.

Before the minute was up, she had decided. "All right. I was told to lead you around for three-quarters of an hour and then give you a letter."

Lies based on the truth are always the most convincing.

"I have the letter in the car."

"You've got ten extra seconds," I said, and let her drop back to earth.

She turned to the car and spent the time getting a small gun out of her handbag.

People turning a gun on you expect some grace time. They expect you to be surprised, which you are. And they expect you to fall back, to recover, to think.

That's where they count on time.

I get surprised. But that makes me quick, not slow.

When she turned her little gun on me, I jumped her. I put my fist around the gun and pulled it out of her hand.

"Who's a naughty girl?" It was a Sauer & Sohn .25. They're about five inches long. "What is a nice girl like you doing with a nasty prewar German popgun like this?" I put it up to her head. "Gonna talk yet or is it gonna be more fun and games?"

"It isn't loaded," she said.

I judged the weight. Six bullets make a difference.

"You don't mind if I pull the trigger, then?"

"Go...go on," she said.

I turned the thing toward a tree and shot a branch off. "I admire your style, miss," I said, "but how you've lived to the ripe old age you have currently attained I don't know." I made her about twenty-seven. "In this day and age, .22s are generally considered more effective than these things."

"You've got to take what you can get, don't you?" she said.

"I don't know," I said. "Do you?"

She resigned herself. She nodded. "That's the way it goes around here. A country girl just doesn't stand a chance when she comes up against a big-city operator like yourself."

They learn to shoot a good line of bull, though.

I turned the gun back on her and frowned. "I'm not too old to learn new tricks," I said. "I've never shot a peppermint-stick woman before, but it seems my best opportunity yet."

Her eyes told me it wasn't quite so much a game anymore.

That was good.

"Who are you? What's this all about? Don't leave out any salient details."

"My name is Mossman. I am a private investigator. About three hours ago a man called my office and hired me to distract you for an hour after you left your hotel. He told me what to say to you to get your interest and said he wanted you out of the way so he could prepare a surprise party for your forty-second birthday. He said there was a hundred dollars in cash outside my office door. I looked while he was on the phone. There was. So I took the job."

"That's it? Dollars?"

"Yes. He had an American voice."

I paused.

"Happy birthday," she said.

CHAPTER XXII

I invited Mossman to leave her car and come back to town with me. One of those invitations the guest finds hard to decline. But to be fair to her, she realized she was into something bigger than she was used to. She sat still in the seat, didn't squirm and didn't talk when I pulled the seat belt tight, and jammed the release mechanism.

I followed the signs to Frome.

I left Mossman in the car in the parking lot.

*   *   *

As soon as I got to my hotel-room door, I knew something was wrong. It was nothing I saw, I'm not the type who leaves little hairs stuck on cracks with spittle. I work by instinct. Hunches, following impulses. Most of the time, that's served me pretty well.

I sensed trouble. I felt it.

I went from my door to Mrs. McKeand's. I almost knocked.

The door was unlocked. I walked straight in.

My client's wife was lying on the bed in a puddle of blood. The blood had been her own. It was a standing pool with a brown scum on top, coagulating. So much had come out of her that it hadn't all been absorbed by the bedclothes. That hadn't kept more from coming out.

She lay on her back. Her head was facing to the

left. But not the simple way. To face her face left, the person who had arranged her had sliced her throat deep and turned the head hard to the right. It went all the way around. It was almost off.

I walked around to look at the face. She had been a pretty woman. But now she even looked innocent, calm. All the acid drained out of her.

But there was little blood on the face. That struck me as strange.

It suggested that the deep cut, the twist, had happened after the body was empty of its blood. Otherwise blood would have spattered up and out on everything through the severed arteries.

I didn't like it. It meant that whoever had done it had had two bites at the cherry. He, or she, had cut arteries elsewhere, then slit her throat, done it deep, then wrenched the head.

It meant no regret. It implied positive involvement in the act of killing. Pleasure.

I stepped away from the body and looked around the room. Drawers were open, the contents were disturbed.

But you don't have to kill a sleeping woman to have a look for something in her room. You don't have to kill her unless you want to.

I didn't like it.

11

"You've been up quite awhile."

"Catching up on the time I lost earlier." Willy smiled. "Yeah, it was quite good."

"Hank giving readers and writer vicarious thrills, spills and delights again?"

"I killed off his client's wife."

"Oh."

"It was a bit grisly."

"With lots of blood, I suppose?"

"Like gravy." He grinned at her.

"I hope you're proud of yourself."

"I didn't do it for fun," he said. "It's a plot requirement." She shrugged.

"Besides, Hank didn't like her. Well, not as a person. So she had to go. I mean, Hank is the hero of the book, isn't he?"

"In addition to being the personification of your worst whims."

"No need to get personal."

"Well, Hank doesn't live a million miles from here."

"I'm not going to fight about it. What's on the agenda?"

"Agenda?"

Willy was slightly irritated. "Don't be obtuse. Plans for evening. Meal here? Is there some visit or visitors I've forgotten about? Or are you out playing bridge with Howard?"

"I would have reminded you. I'm planning to pay some bills and work on the accounts. I didn't know what you might want to do."

"So, nothing." He thought about whether to have a drink.

"I also intended to call Angela."

Which reminded . . . "Hey, did I tell you, I put The Crud into the book?"

"Oh Willy!"

"I've given him a different last name, but it's The Crud all right. He's on the run from the scene of hideous murders."

"Brock can't help being a crud."

"But Angela could help being with Brock."

"Not at this point," Nan said.

"Sure she could."

"If you're going to be like that, I'll tell her you're out."

Willy shrugged. "Charlie said today that I should talk to Deb."

"Oh dear. What about?"

"England. He said she knows about it. I mentioned I was sending Hank there and was getting background info."

"I didn't know Deb knew about England. How's that?"

"Spent some time there in her childhood, he says."

"She probably just had some English boyfriend."

"A lord or a count or something would be the way she would tell it. If she told it."

"What are you going to do?"

"About what?"

"About Deb," Nan said. "Charlie will have told her you're going to call."

"I don't think so. I told him I already had what I needed."

"I bet he does tell her."

"Tough. It's not my problem then."

"He just wants you to get along with her better."

"I don't get along with her badly. I just don't like hoity-toity bitches who think they're better than detective-story writers."

"Don't you think maybe you ought to call her?"

"No."

"All right," Nan said. "I can't make you."

The phone rang.

"You don't think that's Deb, do you?" Willy asked. "Tell her I'm out."

"I'll do no such thing. Besides, it will be Angel. She's going out and wants to talk to us before they leave."

While Willy thought about it, Nan passed him. The phone was on the short wall connecting the living area to the kitchen-eating area of the open-plan ground floor. Willy accepted the decision gracefully and walked through to the living room where they kept their good alcohol on a shelf.

Suddenly he heard anxiety in Nan's voice: "Willy. Willy!"

He came to her quickly.

"It's Lorraine," Nan said. "Lorraine. She wants to talk to you."

"Hello?" Willy said, taking the phone. Asking Nan with his eyes.

Lorraine Brinker was screaming, "They've found Larry!

He's dead! They've found Larry dead!" The screams broke
into sobs and she didn't say any more.

"Hello? Hello? Lorraine?"

There were rustles from handling in his ear. Then another
voice, not frantic but unsteady, said, "Mr. Werth? This is Boo
Brinker. The daughter, you know?"

"Yes, hello, Boo," Willy said. "My God, what's happened?"

"They found Dad's body," Boo said. "He's dead. Mom
wanted you to know. She's pretty upset. Well, you heard. We
all are."

"What happened, Boo?" Willy asked urgently. He felt a
short white-hot panic of mortality.

"They . . . found him." She seemed a little stuck for telling
him what he wanted to know.

"Where?"

"In one of the trailers at the yard."

"In one of the trailers!"

"Yeah."

"Did he . . . Was—was it an accident, or what?"

"Oh, they think he was murdered."

"Murdered! My God. Boo, how awful!"

"Yeah," she said. "Kinda taking some time to sink in, you
know?" She seemed to turn away from the phone for a moment,
then said, "Hey, I gotta go, Mr. Werth. There's this cop here,
but he doesn't seem to know that much about what to do either.
It's all pretty confusing. What?" The question was to someone
at her end. "Oh, Mom says she's sorry for making a ruckus
like she did on the phone just now. She thought she was gonna
be O.K. It's just like, she thought you ought to know 'cause
you were out here last night, she says. Only she's pretty upset.
We all are."

"Of course," Willy said. "My God! My God!"

"I gotta go. She wants me to make some other calls so
people don't hear about it on TV first."

Willy said, "Is there anything we can do to help?" But Boo
had already hung up.

Nan stood silently as Willy turned to her. "Larry Brinker
has been murdered."

"I heard."

Willy didn't know what to think. He didn't know what to
say. He just stood.

"Why?" Nan asked. "Why did it happen?"

Willy shook his head and shrugged. Shock was beginning to overtake him.

"I mean was it robbery or . . . or robbery, or what?"

"I don't know. She didn't say." Willy felt funny. "I think I want to sit down," he said. He turned toward the living room and only then noticed that he was still holding the telephone receiver.

Willy sat in a deep easy chair that was tucked underneath bookshelves. Nan followed uncertainly, and rested, leaning rather than sitting, on the arm of the couch nearby. Willy stared in front of him. He didn't speak.

After waiting for him Nan said, "When you asked about our helping, what did she say?"

"Nothing."

"There must be something."

"She'd started to hang up. She didn't hear."

"Oh," Nan said. "Is there anything—what do you think?"

"I . . . don't know."

"Murdererd," Nan said. "God, it's so strange."

"I know."

"I wonder what the chances are?"

"Of being murdered?"

"Of knowing someone who is murdered. Have you ever known anyone actually murdered?"

"Apart from the ones I kill off myself?" Willy asked. He grimaced at his joke.

"I mean real people."

Willy shook his head. "I killed one this afternoon."

"We can figure it out."

"What?"

"The chances of knowing someone who gets murdered," Nan said. "How many murders happen in this country every year?"

"Twenty thousand or so. That was last year." It was the kind of number Willy knew. "The figures only came out a while ago. Last month."

"And how many people does a person know? A hundred?"

"Oh, more than that."

"I mean personally. Not 'know' in the sense of knowing someone who is assassinated. I mean ones you know, say, to talk to if you pass them in the street."

"It's still going to be more than that. At least two or three hundred. Maybe five hundred, by the time you're our age, with people from the past you don't see now, but still know."

"O.K.," Nan said. "Every murdered person is known by five hundred. If twenty thousand are killed in a year, then the murder victims are known by ten million people. But you've got to allow for foreigners killed here and for people killed being known by the same people. But even if you say the victims are known by only two million, it means that every year about one percent of the American population knows someone who is murdered. Over fifty years, that's one person in two."

"Poor old Larry," Willy said.

Later in the evening, Nan said, "It's time to call Angela."

"Oh, yeah," Willy said. Then, "Should I do it?"

"You? Why?"

"Well, I thought maybe I should be the one to tell her."

"About what?"

"About Larry Brinker."

Nan stared at him. "Why tell her about Larry Brinker?"

"I . . . I just assumed."

"She didn't know him, did she?"

"I don't know. It's just our news. And she knew the daughter, didn't she?"

"Boo was two or three years behind her!"

"Well, I didn't know."

"Well," Nan said, "tell her, by all means, if you want to." She went back to her chair.

Willy got up. "What would she think when she heard it someplace else?"

"How is she going to hear it someplace else? Do you think Indianapolis murders are front-page news in Columbus, Ohio? I don't know why you're making such a point of it."

Hesitating at the phone, Willy asked, "There's no reason I shouldn't tell her, is there?"

"No."

He shrugged, and punched out the number.

The distant receiver rang seven times before being answered. It was a female voice. "Hello."

"Oh, Angel, it's you. I was afraid for a minute there it was going to be The Crud."

"Hello, Daddy! I wondered if you folks might call. Isn't Mom there?"

"She's here. How are you, kid?"

"I'm O.K."

"That bad, huh. And how's The Crud?"

"Cruddy. Daddy, is something wrong? You sound different."

"Well, honey," Willy said, glancing at Nan, "since you ask, yes, we've had some bad news tonight. A friend of ours has been murdered."

"Gosh! How awful for you!"

"Not so much for us, hon, as for his family."

"Of course not, but you must feel terrible! A friend!"

"It was Larry Brinker."

"Who?"

"Larry Brinker. Your mother knows the wife pretty well, Lorraine Brinker, and they had a daughter called Boo you might have known, though she was a couple of years behind you. They live in Castleton."

"I remember a kind of wild kid called Barbara Brinker who went around trying to say shocking things."

"Barbara, yes, that's her name."

"Gee, that's too bad. Awful. Was it robbery or something like that?"

"I don't know any of the details yet, Angel. We only heard tonight. And I just wanted to be the one to tell you, if you were going to hear."

"O.K., thanks."

"How are you, honey? Getting enough to eat?"

Angela took it for what it was, a question about the current success of her husband's business. "I'm eating too much," she said. "Brock says I'm getting fat."

"I'll believe that when I see it."

Nan rose and came to the telephone.

"Why don't you see it, Daddy? Come visit."

"We will one of these days. Only at the moment I'm pretty deep coming up to a deadline."

"Oooo, poor old Mom."

"Speaking of poor old Mom," Willy said, "here she is."

"Can't you sleep?" Nan asked. Having been woken up by his turnings.

"I nearly was," Willy said, "but then I thought of something."

Nan yawned. "What?"

"On the phone Boo Brinker said, 'They think he was murdered.'"

Nan paused. Then, realizing that was it, said, "So?"

"And the other day, yesterday—God, is it only yesterday?—that cop asked those questions about whether Larry was likely to commit suicide."

"Did he?"

"And it just occurred to me that that might be what Boo saying 'They think he was murdered' meant. Instead of saying he was murdered. You see."

"Mmm."

"It might not have been murder at all."

After a pause, sensing that Willy was getting wider awake, Nan sat up. "Willy, what's the difference?"

"Well . . ."

"He's dead, isn't he? There's no question about that."

"I guess not."

"So go to sleep."

"You asked," he said sharply. He sat up beside her. "You spoke first."

"After your thrashings woke me up, sure. I just wondered if there was something you wanted me to do for you, that's all."

He was quiet for a while. "Sorry if I woke you. I was nearly asleep and then I wasn't. Sorry."

"That's all right."

"I'm finding it hard to keep from thinking. Like Angel. When I told her, she said 'How awful for you.' Meaning me or us. I would have thought that was a pretty strange reaction."

"She could probably tell from your voice that you were upset."

"Maybe."

"Besides," Nan said, "we're used to hearing about people being murdered, Angela and I."

"What?"

"You tell us. We've heard about lots and lots of murders."

"But that's totally different."

"Yes," Nan said, "but we've heard the words pretty often. The words aren't as strange to us as they would be in other households, you've got to admit that."

"It's not the same thing at all."

"I didn't say it was," Nan said. Without the energy to press her point.

They were quiet for a bit, and both slid back to lying from sitting.

Nan said, "Are you still there?"

"Yes."

"Do you think Angela might be pregnant?"

"Pregnant?"

"She said Brock said she was getting fat. I felt there was something about the way she said it."

"She told me that, too," he said.

"I think I'll invite them to come over. Brock gets Thursday and Friday off this week because he had to work last weekend. You won't mind, if we keep out of your way. Will you?"

"I don't mind."

"I'll offer to send them the money to come. That will tell how they're doing."

"God, the thought! A little Crud."

"It might be a little Angela."

"Crud spreads. Crud infects. Crud seeps into every facet of human existence."

Nan was silent, but she smiled a little.

12

You don't have to kill a sleeping woman to have a look around her room. So if you kill her it's because you want to.

I didn't like it.

I didn't like it.

I didn't...aaaaah.

It busted my assignment. The vision of British red tape, stiff upper lips, John Bulls. It all meant time, time that I didn't have.

What did I have? Maybe six or seven hours to be out of the country. How do I decide that?

I left Stella McKeand as I found her. I went to my room, her room first, and put the "Do Not Disturb" sign out. Then I went to my room. I packed my bag. I left some money for the bill in an envelope in the toilet, on the toilet, damn it. I put my own "Do Not Disturb" sign out. I walked out of the hotel to the telephone booths in the middle of town. I called the airport to get the times of planes back to the States.

Then it was a matter of how to spend the time I had left in Frome. Catching murderers.

I went back to my car, where I'd left Mossman.

She was gone.

No, she wasn't, too much trouble.

I opened the door and slugged her in the mouth. "You stupid cunt," I said, even thought I won't say it next draft. "That's for doing what Americans ask you to for money without asking questions."

Holding her bleeding lip, she looked hurt. That's when I knew she was special.

"My client's wife has been murdered. What do you know about it?"

"Murdered?"

"Yeah," I said, "with her throat cut and

55

13

Nan could see something was wrong, not only by the fact that Willy was downstairs but by the way he came down.

And he knew she knew.

"It's just not there," he said. "I can't concentrate. Nothing flows. The words don't fit together." He walked through to the living-room window. He stood and looked out without seeing much that was outside his mind.

"Is something wrong, Will?"

"It's goddamn Larry Brinker. I can't get him out of my head, the poor bastard. It's not that I know him—knew him—that well. How many times have I seen him this year? Five? Six? But my head keeps coming back to him."

Willy paused; Nan said nothing.

He turned to her. "I mean what the hell business do I have all of a sudden remembering that he wore tinted contact lenses to make his eyes bluer? I've got no business wasting time on things like that when I have a deadline to meet and bills to pay. Do I? Huh?"

"You can't help what you think," Nan said when she realized he expected her to respond. "If it affects you, it affects you."

"All I could do was have Hank bash a woman in the mouth because I didn't feel like making the effort to stick with the plot line I had planned."

"What was he supposed to do to her?"

"It wasn't like that." Annoyed. "She was going to get away. He was going to go into the hotel restaurant and order some cereal. I was going to have him ask for Cheerios 'cause they won't have them over there. Then she was going to come back and find him."

"He likes her?"

"He will. And he'll be sad when she dies. But I just couldn't make the effort to move my fingers and spend the time. I just don't feel like it, you know?"

She nodded.

"And I remember another time," Willy said. "I ran into him in a deli on the South Side, you know, Shapiro's."

Nan realized he was talking about Larry Brinker again.

"We saw each other in the line and ended up eating together. He ate his pickles backhand off a fork instead of just picking them up with his fingers like the rest of us. Now why the hell should I be remembering stuff like that?"

Suddenly Willy marched away from the window and dropped heavily onto the couch. "I get pretty tired of myself sometimes. My head gets tired."

"It's all a shock," Nan said.

"I'll tell you what it is," Willy said. "I feel involved." Then, again, "I feel involved."

There were no cars in front of the Brinkers' house, so Willy parked on the road. He walked quickly to the front door, not wanting to lose the drift of his decision to act, his decision to attack his preoccupation instead of suffering from it. He rang the bell sharply. He waited by looking across the street at the nearby houses on the hill. An amiably developed section of the city, with large plots and mature trees.

He was turning to ring again when the door opened.

"Oh!" he said, surprised into uncertainty.

In front of him stood a spectacularly good-looking girl of nineteen or twenty. She was barefoot, in white shorts and a white knit shirt. "Yes?"

"I . . . uh."

"Do you want something, mister?"

"I thought . . . isn't this the Brinkers' house?" Willy looked for the number to see if he could possibly have made a mistake.

"Yeah." She looked at him. "Do I know you?"

He tried to think. "You're not Boo?"

"Oh, yes, I am!"

"I didn't expect you to be so . . . life-size."

The girl rubbed some sleep from the corner of her eye onto the bridge of her nose.

"You've . . . I haven't . . . My name is William Werth. You . . . We talked on—"

"On the phone. Right," she interrupted. "I remember, but, God, I don't recognize you at all. Did I ever meet you? I bet I couldn't have, 'cause I would have remembered a distinguished-looking guy like you are."

"Oh . . ."

"You're the one who writes stuff, aren't you?" Boo asked.

"Yes, I am. I do," Willy said. "Detective novels."

"Aromatic! That's a real great rip-off." She smiled at him and nodded with chaste approval. "Hey, do you want to come in?"

Willy walked into the hall.

"Did you want to see Mom or something?"

"I . . . uh, was really thinking that I might see the, uh, Sergeant Hearns."

"That's the head cop on the case, right?"

"Yes. Only—since his car isn't here . . ."

"He hasn't been out here today. He must be doing whatever he's doing in town. What did you want to see him about?"

"Well, I know it's not really much of my business, but—"

"You wanted to find out how he's doing about who killed Dad, is that it?"

"Mostly, yes, I guess it is."

"Hey, it's great of you to take an interest like that. That's really nice. You must be really busy and all, and even so you take the time to come out here like that."

"I . . . I . . ." Willy was distinctly disturbed by Boo's appearance. "As well as keeping up to date with it, I half hoped, thought—well, that maybe I might be able to help him."

"How?" Boo asked sharply.

"Well . . ." Willy was upset that what he was about to say would sound weak. "It would depend on the facts, of course. I don't really know much about it yet. But I thought I might be able to help more than most people—members of the public, I mean. Because of what I do for a living. I spend a lot of time thinking about—well, this kind of thing. I might be able to do something small, follow up some lead that they wouldn't have the time, the manpower to follow up themselves." He felt exposed.

"You want to help," Boo said with warmth. "That's really cool."

For having that reaction, he thanked her. He felt suddenly better.

"If I'd thought more carefully, I'd have known Hearns wouldn't be here. He'll be at where your father was found. That was his place of business, wasn't it?"

"Dad sold trailers. He was left in one of them."

It sounded a stark summary of the fate of a man to Willy. His face showed it. But Boo shrugged. "Facts are facts," she said.

"When was he killed, Boo?"

"Sunday night. They didn't find him till Tuesday. That's why Mom was all freaked out. The worry and all that. I came in Monday late 'cause he was missing."

"Who found him?"

"They have a cleaning lady at the site comes in twice a week to clear up all the display trailers. She found him."

Shaking his head, thinking of Lorraine Brinker, Willy said, "Dear, oh dear, oh dear."

Suddenly Boo chuckled, then tried to control herself and ended up shaking for a while. "Jesus, I shouldn't be laughing," she said. "But I couldn't help it. You sounded so much like an old mother hen saying dear, oh dear, and like that." She controlled herself again.

Willy felt attacked. He stiffened, and in finding it hard to find words he showed too clearly what he felt.

"Hey, I'm really sorry," Boo said, and put a hand on his arm. "I just say what comes into my head, you know. I always have. I'm immature that way. Inside this I'm only six, I guess."

Willy asked, "How is your mother taking it all?"

"She's been sleeping a lot, thanks to the quack. She's in pretty bad shape really. Yeah. Well, she's got to be, doesn't she?"

"I think I better go now," Willy said.

"Oh. O.K."

He walked the few steps back to the door. "I'll keep you informed of what I find out," he said, rather too portentously. He tried to make it less significant. "That is, if you want me to." But it didn't work.

"Oh yeah. That'd be great," Boo said.

"How long will you be in Indianapolis?"

"God, I don't know. Maybe for a while, the way things are going. Back in the city—oh, sorry, New York—I was kinda between jobs, as they say. I don't really know. Maybe it won't be all that long."

"What . . ." Willy said. "What kind of work do you do? In New York."

"Oh, I'm an actress and model. Actress, mostly. I made a movie last winter. Didn't Mom tell you?"

"I knew your father better than your mother," Willy said. Then, after a clumsy pause, "But if you act half as good as you look, you must have quite a future."

Her face lit up like a sunlamp. "God, that's real sweet of

you to say, Mr. Werth. I always thought I was kind of too flash-looking for hometown kinda people, 'cause I only really blossomed when I went away. But that may be part of getting to know the world better, you know what I mean."

Willy nodded, but didn't quite know what she meant. He saluted and went through the door.

While he was on the path, Boo called from the doorway, "Goodbye!" Without turning back, Willy waved and concentrated on sliding smoothly, easily, gracefully into the seat of his car.

By then, when he did look back, she was gone.

Willy went to look for Hearns at Brinkers' Mobile Homes.

In trailer row on West Washington Street, Brinker's was a relatively large lot with a high link fence enclosing a village of aluminum and windows. There was one car in the parking lot, not recognizably a police car.

The business office was brick and wheelless. Signs in its windows bragged about a variety of mobile living, working and recreation units.

Inside, a man, apparently in his fifties, with coiffured white hair, sat at a table next to three desks and some filing cabinets. There was an air of steady business about the objects in the room. There was an air of no business about the man, who concentrated on the *Star* sports page and was slow to acknowledge Willy's presence.

"Oh," he said, finally. He rose from the chair but didn't decide where to go.

"Don't get up," Willy said with formality. "I'm not a customer. I'm looking for Detective Sergeant Hearns."

"Oh," the man said, with recognition. "He hasn't been here today. In fact, nobody's been here today. Not even the people who work here." The man walked to Willy's side of the table, then sat on it. "What can I do for you? More questions? I think I told him just about everything I could yesterday. Or is it one of these 'Let's go through it all again' routines?"

With rising pleasure, Willy realized he'd been mistaken for a policeman. It was a bubbly feeling, and he found it hard to keep from smiling. He coughed into his hand and turned away. He turned back, under some control, to find a puzzled face watching his.

"There's a water cooler if you want a drink."

"I would, yes," Willy said. The man pointed it out, and the drink was calming.

"It's not that I mind going through it all again, don't get me wrong. There's no rush for R.V.s anyway just at the moment, with the gas thing like it is."

"R.V.s?"

"Recreational Vehicles. Ones for fun, not to live in."

"Oh."

"But I'll tell you, I think your Hearns is on a wrong track worrying so much about that hippie kid."

"You do, huh?"

"Yeah," a bit belligerently. "Just because a guy has long hair"—he rubbed his own head—"and has a bit of hassle about the price he's being offered for his trailer doesn't mean he's going to off and kill somebody."

"No . . ." Willy said cautiously. "But hassle is hassle."

"I know, but hell's bells, this is a business. I've seen it lots of times one way and another. This one, a kid comes in with his girl and a trailer he bought here that he's spray-painted with flowers and stuff. And he gets mad because the boss says the paint job makes it worth less instead of more. Well, the guy's spent hours on a thing like that and wouldn't be selling it if he didn't need the loot. He's bound to get a little heat on when he heard the birds and the bees. So when you get heated you say things you don't mean. I mean that's just business. It doesn't happen every day but it happens."

"What did the kid say?"

"Just that Brinker was a crook and if that's the way he treated customers he was going to starve to death and good riddance. Then Brinker told him what he could do with his trailer. And the kid left."

"When was this?"

"Late afternoon, Sunday. About my knocking-off time."

"The same day," Willy said carefully, "that Mr. Brinker got knocked off?"

"Oh well, poor choice of words."

"The kid was the only customer Mr. Brinker had trouble with recently?"

"Yeah, I guess so. He was pretty much a gentleman. He liked a bit of style about the place. He didn't usually have trouble, you know?"

"I've not asked your name," Willy said.

"Barry Youngman."

"And if you think the hippie kid is the wrong track, do you have any ideas about who might be the right track?"

"Naw, I don't know anything about it, except that it shocked the hell out of me."

"Are you the only employee, Mr. Youngman?"

"Oh, no. There are two other full time. Shifty—or, rather, Sam—Shilton, and The Kid—that's Neil Tudge."

"And a cleaner," Willy said, with a little smile.

"Oh yeah."

"So," looking around, "where is everybody today?"

"Shifty called in sick. The kid didn't show up. But there's nothing much to do here."

"I see," Willy said. "The body was found in one of the trailers?"

"Yeah."

"Can I have a look?"

"It's O.K. by me."

"Which one was it?"

"Come on." Locking the office door behind them, Youngman led Willy to a long white paneled trailer on blocks at the back of the lot.

"It's a pretty fancy one for having to be towed, isn't it?"

"Oh yeah," Youngman said. "One of the best. Good for being set up permanently on a site."

"Sell many?"

"None since I came."

"How long have you had this job?"

"About eighteen months." Youngman thought a moment. "Sixteen months."

"It's not so common to be changing jobs at your age," Willy said. "What did you do before?"

"I've done quite a few things," Youngman said carefully. "But I know R.V.s and I'm settled here. Or at least I was."

"Is there a high turnover of salesmen in this business?"

"Usually guys either stay one place forever or they move around a lot."

Willy nodded. He tried the door of the trailer. It wouldn't open. "Can you unlock it for me?"

Youngman looked surprised. "Don't you have the key?"

"Me? No."

"The cop took everybody's keys to it. Oh, sorry. Sergeant

Hearns. I figured you had a key off him when you said you wanted to see around."

"I'm going to have to find Hearns," Willy said.

"Guess so."

"Still, I'll have a little look."

"Suit yourself."

Willy inspected the trailer, trying to see in through each window. All had curtains or Venetian blinds, partially obscuring the interior. Willy saw some table surfaces and a couch, but nothing clearly.

Youngman saw Willy frowning about the windows. "It's policy," he said. "Except for three or four at the front, we keep all the blinds and curtains drawn. We tell people it's to keep upholstery from fading in the sun, but mostly it's so people can't see much without having a salesman there ready with a pitch."

"Are they kept locked?"

"Usually. Same reason. All the salesmen have keys. Except when cops take them." Suddenly Youngman straightened.

"What's wrong?"

"Telephone," he said. "I hear the phone ringing." He turned and jogged back to the office.

Willy didn't hear anything until the office door opened, but then the ringing was clear. He walked slowly along the path the salesman had covered more quickly, but before he had to decide whether to go to the car or into the office again, Youngman reappeared.

"Missed it," he said. "Don't know how long it was ringing. We've got an outside bell, but it's broken. It's hard to know whether I should have it fixed on my own authority or just let it ride. You haven't heard anything about what's going to happen to this place, have you?" Willy shook his head. "Do you know who I should call? It's hard on them and all that, but things ought to be decided pretty soon."

"You could try calling the house," Willy said. "The daughter is there and seems to be doing things like answering the phone and the door. At least she could tell you who is handling things."

"O.K.," Youngman said.

"Do you know the Brinker family?"

"Not really. Mrs. Brinker came in a couple times a month." He shrugged his shoulders.

Willy started to leave, but hesitated. "How long has that

outdoor bell been out of order?"

"Three, four days. Maybe five. Why? Think it might be important?"

"Could be," Willy said. "Did it go out of order often?"

"Never before since I've been here."

"Interesting," Willy said. He got into his car and left Barry Youngman scratching his bottom with one hand and his head with the other.

"Hello?"

"It's me. I'm just calling to say I won't be home for lunch. I'm in town and I'll catch something here."

"I was just going out anyway."

"I've been playing policeman," Willy said with a certain glee.

"Policeman?"

"I went to try to find this police sergeant, Hearns, at Larry Brinker's trailer place, and the salesman there mistook me for a cop. I didn't disabuse him and I wandered around for half an hour asking coplike questions."

"How do you know what coplike questions are?" Nan asked ungraciously.

"Come on!" he said.

More warmly she said, "I can hear you're pleased with yourself."

"I guess I am. It's got my blood running, for what that's worth."

"Don't get yourself in trouble, Willy."

"What kind of trouble?"

"Impersonating a police officer, or . . . something like that."

"But I didn't impersonate a police officer. He didn't ask, that's all."

"Well . . ." Still doubtful.

"But I didn't call about that. I just wanted to let you know I won't be home till later."

"Are you going to work this afternoon?" His conscience.

"I'll give it a go later. But it didn't exactly flow this morning."

"I know," she said.

"Oh yeah. You were there."

"Charlie called."

"What did he want?"

"He didn't say. But he was pretty short with me."

"Short?"

"You know, sort of not friendly."

"Probably just in a hurry or something. Am I supposed to stop in, or call him back, or what?"

"He didn't say."

"Oh."

"I think it has something to do with Deb."

"Deb? What about Deb?"

"I don't know."

"What did he say?"

"Nothing, honestly. Nothing about her at all. It's just a feeling. But I bet I'm right."

"Just what I need," Willy said. "Any other messages?"

"No."

"No publisher harassment?"

"No, nothing, Willy."

"O.K., hon. See you later."

"You will call Charlie, won't you? Don't let it get lost."

Willy spent forty-five minutes over a light lunch. His thoughts were heavy, a battle framed between whether he should risk embarrassment by going back to police headquarters in order to seek Hearns to declare his interest, or whether he should slide around it all and work alone on the case for a while.

A Hank would work alone, but for Willy propriety triumphed and after paying his bill he walked to police headquarters. He presented himself at the information counter and he was vastly relieved not to recognize any of the uniformed men behind it. The man he had humiliated himself before was absent. It added to his rising sense that it was one of those days in which all things go well.

Willy asked a weather-beaten but young officer for Hearns. "It's about the Brinker case," he said.

The officer stared at Willy for a moment. Then he lifted a telephone and made a call. "Someone is coming down to see to you," he said. "You want a chair?"

"Thanks, no. I'll stand."

Many people got off the elevators and walked toward the door before a man in a rumpled blue jacket and loosened tie stopped at the information counter and had Willy pointed out to him.

"You're looking for Hearnsie about the Brinker killing, that right?"

"That's exactly right."

"You wanna come with me?"

"Where to?"

"Upstairs, for crying out loud. You don't think I'm gonna stand around here in the goddam public lobby talking about a murder case, do you?"

"Lead and I shall follow," Willy said, with some annoyance at the man's seeming lack of awareness that the pursuit of justice should raise people involved in it above pettinesses.

"You some kind of nut?"

"Aren't we all?"

The man looked at him as if he were some kind of nut. But led Willy to an elevator.

Willy asked, "Are we going to the detective room?"

"That's usually where you find detectives."

"Is it still E446?"

The rumpled cop faced him, though the elevator doors behind opened. "You been there before, huh? Know your way around, huh? So why do you make me waste my time coming down here to pick you up?"

"I didn't ask for a guide," Willy said. The elevator doors closed. "The guy at the desk sent for you."

The man shrugged and turned away again to punch the button.

"But I've never been upstairs here before," Willy said.

"So what's with the E446?"

"I've got a floor plan of the Police Department, but it's pretty old. I know they've moved Communications to the third floor. I just wondered whether Homicide and Robbery was still in the same place."

"How come you have a plan of this place?" The questions were no longer hostile, however. Mild curiosity, to pass the brief time before he could get back to what he wanted to be doing.

"A friend got me one," Willy answered non-communicatively.

"You got a friend. I got friends, but they don't get me Police Department floor plans. I mean, that's a pretty weird thing to ask a friend to get."

"I guess so."

"So why are you?"

"I'm a writer," Willy said.

"Ahhh," the man said, as if it explained everything. Only meaning that it didn't. "So you're a writer. What the hell do you write about floor plans?"

The elevator came again. This time they got in. Three other people got in with them.

Willy said, "I write detective novels." The rumpled cop paid less attention than the other three people.

Though aware he was forcing the subject, Willy continued, "And sometimes it's handy to know where things are inside buildings like the Police Department."

The man showed no reaction, but as they got out of the elevator he turned Willy to the left and said, "I didn't know there were floor plans here."

"Oh yes. They're distributed to new recruits to show them where all the fire hoses and extinguishers are."

"Oh yeah?" the man asked, devoid of further curiosity.

They walked the short corridor in silence, and turned in to the Homicide and Robbery with Violence reception room where the man said, "Guy for Hearns."

"Take a seat, please," the reception officer said.

"I'd rather stand, thanks."

The rumpled cop left without looking back.

After standing for five minutes Willy asked, "Can you tell me how long it's going to be?"

"Sergeant Hearns is expected any minute. It won't be long."

Willy sat down. It was another twenty-three minutes. It seemed very long.

"I hear you want to see me," Hearns said when he finally appeared in the reception office. He squinted at Willy. "I know you, don't I?"

"I met you at—"

Hearns interrupted, "That guy's house in Castleton, Brinker."

"That's right."

Hearns seemed to think about it. "Just what did you want to tell me?"

Willy looked around uneasily. Hearns didn't respond. Willy said, "Isn't there somewhere else we can talk?"

"If you want. Come on."

Willy followed Hearns along a latticework between desks and populated chairs to a row of offices. Hearns opened the door to one. "Looks empty," he said. "Go on in. I'll be there in a sec."

Willy walked in and sat on a wooden chair in front of the desk.

Hearns reappeared almost immediately with a pad of paper, which he dropped onto the desk top as he went to sit behind it. He took out a pen. "O.K., Mr. Werth."

"You know my name," Willy observed.

"It's not a secret, is it?"

"No."

"You told me at the Brinker house. I'm good at what I do; I remember. You want to talk to me. What about?"

"About the Brinker murder."

"Did I ever tell you he was murdered?" Hearns asked quietly.

"Well, no."

"So why do you say 'murder'? You come in to confess?"

"Certainly not."

"What a pity. I'll have to keep working on the case then." Willy looked puzzled. Hearns smiled. "Don't get me wrong," he continued. "It is a murder case. I'm just fussy about people jumping to conclusions."

"That's a very reasonable attitude," Willy said. "I'm sorry."

"So what's up?"

Willy felt markedly less certain of his ground. "It's a little hard to express."

"Try," Hearns said.

"Well, I wanted to know how the case was getting on. Whether you had leads you were following, or what?"

"I am also," Hearns said, "more than a little fussy about discussing my cases with members of the public."

"That's the thing," Willy said. "I don't think I'm just an ordinary member of the public."

Hearns stared unreactingly, as if to say "You look pretty ordinary to me."

"Well, I am, but not in the usual way." Willy tried to sort out a beginning. "I write detective novels. I've been at it since 1950, so I have a different outlook on murders and solving them from most people. More experience thinking about . . . well, situations like this, more than the man in the street. And what with my knowing Larry Brinker and a bit about his family, I thought I might be in a unique position to help. You see?"

Hearns said nothing.

"I know how busy police officers are. I keep up with the statistics and with police journals. It seemed to me that there might be things that I could do that you or your men might not have the time to do yourselves. I thought I might be in a position to offer help, to expedite the solution of the crime."

Hearns absorbed this for a moment, and then said, "Buzz off, Mr. Werth."

"Excuse me?"

"You're a fly around dead meat. Buzz off. You're wasting my time."

"I don't think that—"

"If something needs to be done, I'll do it. If I don't do it, it doesn't need to be done. I don't honestly give a damn what you read and write. We're not at the point of taking voluntary contributions from self-seeking people who make up stories."

Willy was horrified at being called self-seeking. "I'm not—"

"You're telling me you're not here for research for some fairy tale or other? Well, tell me what you like. If we want help, we go to people who deal in facts. If you have any facts I should know, tell me. Otherwise, go away so I can get on with my work."

"All right. Do you know—" Willy began, and already felt trapped into an irrelevance that he had to finish.

"What?" Hearns asked.

"That the Brinkers' daughter was involved in making a pornographic film."

"Involved?"

"Starred in," Willy said.

"Here? She made it in Indianapolis?"

"No. New York."

Hearns rubbed his chin and looked as if he were cogitating. "Should I ask just what this has to do with the price of contortionists, or am I supposed to know?"

"Well, I don't know exactly. But it's one of those fringe bits of information that might just fit a piece in. That's why I asked you how things stood at the beginning. I might be able to fit something in."

"Your imagination must be a great professional asset, Mr. Werth."

"And also, I don't understand what Larry was doing in the trailer he was found in. Back from the road, after hours. I mean, if it was paperwork, he had an office for that and there was no need to use a luxurious trailer—"

Hearns rose with finality. "Get out, Mr. Werth."

Willy stood involuntarily and began to retreat as Hearns came around from behind the desk.

"Let me give you some advice. No, I'll give you an order. Keep out of it, Mr. Werth. Do you understand me?"

Willy retreated to the reception room. Behind him he heard Hearns say, "Smith, could you show Mr. Werth the shortest way out of the building? I'd do it myself, but I'd be too tempted to have him use a window."

14

I decided to leave Stella McKeand as I found her. I carried her "Do Not Disturb" sign by its edges to her door. Deftly I slipped it on the handle and left her.

I went to my room, packed my bag and put some money in an envelope on the bed. I like to pay my debts to people in business, if not to society. I put my own "Do Not Disturb" sign out and carried my bag through the hotel lobby to the sidewalks in the middle of town. I got a phone booth in front of the post office and called the airport to get times of planes back to the States.

Then it was a matter of deciding how to spend the time I had left in Frome.

I walked to my car. Where I'd left Mossman.

She was sitting where she'd been left. I put the bag in the trunk and my fist in her face.

"You dumb broad," I said. "That's what you get for doing what Americans pay you to do without asking questions."

Holding her bleeding lip, she looked hurt.

"My client's wife has been murdered. What do you know about it?"

"Murdered?"

I got into the car. I was in the driver's seat. "You tell me what is going on," I told her, "or I'll gift-wrap you and drop you with a note pinned to your tits on the door of the police station."

"They wouldn't know how to get the note off," she said.

"They can't be half as dumb and nasty as the cops back home. I could tell you things about them that would make your hair curl. They think that they're the only ones who know anything. They think they're the only ones who understand why people do things, they're the only ones who can understand what's happened at the scene of a crime and why something took place. They're rude to members of the public even though they are meant to be serving the public and the public pays their wages. They're rude, they're crude, they're obtuse and they can't see their own eyelids. They're short and fat and ugly and have webbed feet. They're so stupid they think that sperm is white and urine is yellow just to help them tell whether they're coming or going. They're so illiterate they never read my books and probably only learn how to be cops from shows on television.

Oh, hell.

15

"Oh, you're home."

"Yes," Willy said.

"I saw the car but I didn't hear anything. I thought you might be out for a walk."

"Of course I'm home," Willy said. "It's where I live."

Nan stiffened at the unexpected attack, then said, "What's wrong, hon?"

"Nothing important. I've got a deadline to meet and I can't work, that's all."

"Oh," she said.

"It's not the kind of thing that happens to me."

"You . . . didn't work this afternoon?"

"I spent some time upstairs at the typewriter, yes. Work, no."

Nan decided. "I'm going to have a beer. Do you want one?"

"No."

"Pop?"

"What flavor?"

"Oh, Pepsi, lemon . . ."

"Oh, never mind. I don't feel like one." He rubbed the back of his neck. "Changed my mind, such as it is. It's this Larry Brinker thing. I can't think properly."

The telephone rang. Nan was pouring beer into a glass. Willy answered it. "Hello."

"William?" It was a woman's voice with a formal tone.

"Yes?"

"I hope I haven't interrupted your work."

"Who is this?"

"Deborah. Your sister-in-law." Some offense had been taken.

"Oh, hello, Deb."

"Charles said that you wanted a little help with the whatever that you are trying to write at the moment. He said you wanted to talk to me."

"He did?"

"He said it was about the interstices of English life."

"Oh," Willy said.

"You don't sound very enthusiastic."

"Don't I?"

"Did Charles get it wrong, William? Are you not including a section in England in your current work?"

"I've sent Hank over there for a bit, but he won't be staying long."

"Well, what is it that you want my help with then?"

"That's, uh, a little hard to say."

"Is it?" Deb asked coolly.

"Well, yes."

"Why?"

"I didn't expect to be talking to you. I mean just now, and I haven't got my head clear enough to be able to sort out the kind of things I want to know."

"So you don't want to talk to me."

"Well, if it's all the same to you, not just now."

"I'm very sorry to have disturbed you, William," Deb said without an iota of sorrow.

"Look, Deb, if you can—" he began, but she hung up. Willy stood holding the telephone dumbbell in his hand, feeling like one. "Hell."

"What did she want? Willy?" Nan asked, with some concern.

"It's her pushy husband."

"Surely it was Deb on the phone?"

"Oh yeah. But Charlie was behind that calamity."

"What calamity?"

"Oh, give it a rest, will you? It's too complicated to go into."

"I am well aware that you are under strain," Nan said firmly, "but I'm not going to be snapped at for no good reason. If you don't want to talk to me, that's fine, but I expect communication with me to be in a civil manner."

Willy turned for escape toward the living room but found himself wrapped in telephone wire. He turned around and hung it up.

Nan brought an open can of beer as he sat staring through the picture window. He took it and sipped.

After a few minutes, Willy turned to her and was about to speak when the telephone rang.

Smiling with the small irony of Willy and the world both

deciding to speak at once, Nan rose and answered.

"Hello?"

In response to the voice at the other end, her voice took on a reflected urgency. "Oh! Charlie! Why, yes, he is. Is something the matter?" Covering the mouthpiece she called Willy. "It's Charlie and he says it's very important."

Willy shook his head violently. "I don't want to talk to him, I don't want to."

"It's too late. I've already told him you're here."

For several seconds Willy didn't move.

Nan whispered, "I am not going to be put in the middle. You will answer this telephone." To Charlie, she said, "He's just coming."

Willy came.

"Hello?"

"Why the hell did you have to go and shit on Deb when she called you, William? There was just no need for that, no need at all. You must know what it cost her to call you, knowing that you hate her like you do. You must have known she only did it because I asked her to do it as a favor to you, to help you on your goddamn book. So why do you have to crap on her when she's only trying to help, that's what I want to know. Why?"

"I never asked you to get her to call me, Charlie, and besides today—"

"Don't play the semanticist with me. You crapped on her for no good reason. Just don't come to me for help again, sonny. It's not good enough, brother. You can take your goddamn book and stuff it up your goddamn ass."

"Look, Charlie, I'm having problems and—"

"You're breaking my heart." Charlie hung up.

Willy returned the receiver to its carriage.

"Did he hang up on you?" Nan asked.

"Yup."

"What did he say?"

"He said I wasn't civil to Deb."

After a hesitation Nan said, "What are you going to do?"

"About what? Deb and Charlie?"

"And about work."

"It's so hard to concentrate. It's the same reason I couldn't talk to Deb, just talk her along and ask her questions whether I used the answers or not. I'm not in the book, all of a sudden." He bent his head into his hands. "I don't know, I don't know."

"I thought," Nan said candidly, "that we'd got through these days a long time ago." Willy didn't react. "You'll do whatever you have to."

"The problem," Willy said, facing her again, "is identifying what I have to do."

"You have to try, at least," she said.

"I suppose so."

Having little else in mind to do, Willy rose to go to the stairs to his office. He hesitated at the bottom, and during that moment Nan said, "Willy?"

"Yeah?"

"Oh . . . never mind."

"What?"

"Nothing."

"What did you want, Nan?"

"It's . . . well, I have to ask. It's nothing to do with me, is it?"

"What?"

"This distraction. I've not upset you somehow, done something?"

"You? What have you got to do with the price of contortionists?"

"Well, I—"

"Women think they're the center of the universe," Willy said tiredly. He went upstairs.

But he didn't work. Instead he read the newspapers, the Indianapolis siblings, morning *Star* and afternoon *News*.

The stories on Larry Brinker were virtually identical, and provided a little information that Willy did not already have. Larry had been shot and found dead in a trailer at his business. Police offered no public hypothesis. There were no signs of a struggle; nothing was apparently missing.

Willy cut both articles out. He filed them under "Miscellaneous Crime Clips." He thought for a moment, then took them out and started a new folder.

Willy's office occupied one of the house's four bedrooms. It was a warren of work surfaces, shelves, storage boxes, filing cabinets and useful places. Notes with ideas, clippings of conceivable interest, pieces of paper with any impulsive connection or attraction were all saved, along with records of his writing and non-writing activites. He also kept corrected drafts of books published and rough drafts of all the unpublished work he had ever done. In practice the files provided few sparking points. Day-to-day ruminations were more likely to find themselves converted into text. But the twist for *Hayride Horror* came from an old clipping, when it came, and the records and files gave Willy a sense of security. When he felt dry of ideas, he knew he had boxes and shelves dripping with them.

Willy immersed himself for a while. He read an article on police suicides.

Then he took the telephone. It rang several times before it was answered, finally, by Boo.

"Is that Barbara?" Willy asked.

"Yes. Who's that?"

"This is Willy Werth."

There was a pause. "Oh! The writer."

"That's right."

"I didn't recognize you," Boo said.

Willy said, "I noticed."

"It was because you're old but your voice sounds so young on the phone. I was trying to think which of the guys I know called Willy could possibly have such a sexy voice."

Willy found it hard to follow that.

"Do you want to talk to Mother?"

"No," Willy said. "I want to talk to you. What I'd like to do is come out to the house and see you for a few minutes, if that's all right."

"Gee, when?"

"Now, if you're free. About your father."

"Oh. Oh, well." She thought. "What about Dad? Has something happened?"

"Not exactly. Not really. But I'd like to come out and talk to you in person."

"Well, O.K. then."

"Is now convenient?"

"Well . . . yeah, I guess."

"It shouldn't take very long, but I feel it's important."

"Oh, that's O.K., Mr. Werth. See you."

Downstairs Nan was making food. Smiling, she said, "Did the smell distract you? I thought I'd make something you like to cheer you up a bit."

"Oh, Christ," Willy said. "Dinner. I forgot."

"Forgot!"

"It's just, I'm going out for a while. Just a bit. Will it keep?"

She scowled at him. "If a cat doesn't get it where I'm going to put it."

"Sorry."

"Where are you going?"

"Out to the Brinkers'."

"The Brinkers'? What does Lorraine want? I didn't hear the phone ring."

"It didn't. It . . . it's the only time I can go out. It's not convenient for them later."

"What's happening?"

"I need to talk some things over with them, about Larry."

"It's nothing to do with you, Willy!"

"Yes and no," Willy said.

"No and no! You're not a policeman. You're a writer, that's all. And one with commitments to fulfill."

"It's sort of an investment in—"

"That is stupid!" she said.

"I feel I should follow my interests—"

"Compulsions!"

"Well, I can't help it," he said. She nodded severely because he had damned himself. "It's where what I write about comes out of, deep down. I've got to do things that I have to do."

Nan turned away. As he left the house, Willy heard her banging the lid on the stewpot.

Boo answered the door. "Come in, Mr. Werth."

They went into the living room; Boo dropped to the floor and Willy sat on an antique straight-backed chair. With a start he remembered that he had meant to ask Larry about antiques. For Hank. He felt a kind of sinking confusion of images, intentions, memories.

"Isn't that chair comfortable, Mr. Werth?"

"No, it's O.K."

"It's one of Dad's old ones. I don't know if it was supposed to be sat on even when they made it, but it sure never fit my bottom."

Willy realized that Hank wouldn't be uncovering the details of the antique scam the way he'd originally planned. That asking Larry would have been a waste of time. That his book was going to finish up short.

"Uh, what was it that you wanted, Mr. Werth?"

Brought back to his task.

"In a way, Boo—oh, may I call you Boo?"

"Everybody does," she said, "even you."

"Uh," he said. He was self-conscious but said easily enough, "And I'm Willy."

"O.K."

"In a way, Boo, I ought to be talking to your mother."

"I can get her if you want. She's mostly a lot better."

"Well, no. I was going to say, but as you are here and are taking care of the business side of things, it's just as well that I talk to you."

"Oh, if it's a business thing, Daddy's lawyer, Mrs. Cunningham, is handling that kind of thing."

"No, it's not business," Willy said. He felt slightly irritated.

"Uh, well," Boo said in the pause, "what is it?"

"I suppose you know that the Indianapolis Police Department, like all or almost all police departments in the country, is undermanned."

"Is it?"

"It is. And that means that however much they might want to follow up all the ramifications of each case they handle, they aren't always—or even ever—really able to investigate a case completely thoroughly. Each detective has to work on several cases at once, and although it isn't as unmanageable as it sounds, because of inevitable lapses of time in the work on any one case, it still means that many cases—I'd even say most—don't get investigated the way they might be, or even should be."

Boo shifted on the floor. When she became aware that he had finished speaking, she asked, "Was that what you wanted, Mr. Werth?"

"Willy, please," Willy said. He was more expansive since he had completed his run-up. At last.

"O.K."

"Thing is, you know, I'm a writer."

"I know. You said."

"But not just a general writer, even of fiction, but a writer of detective and what is generally called crime fiction, and though it's fiction, it means that in a certain way I have a lot of experience in areas like what happened to your father. Not, I must assure you, that this sort of thing happens often to my friends and acquaintances. This is certainly the first time."

"I don't want to be impolite," Boo said, "but I'm going out in a minute."

"Ah," Willy said. "Are you? All right. I won't be a minute. But I thought it was important that I give you some of the background about why I was thinking what I'm thinking, you see."

He paused, but she didn't speak.

"Because of—no, I won't give reasons again," smiling to show he understood she was in a hurry. "What I wanted to know is whether I can have your authorization, your family's authorization, to supplement the police investigation of your father's death. That's basically it."

For a moment Boo didn't take it in. Not quite paying attention, she said, "You want my O.K. to do what? Help the police?"

"That's it, pretty much, yes." Willy smiled.

"Why? Aren't the police doing it right?"

"Oh, it's not that. But as I tried to suggest, they've got lots of cases, and if I help, I might look into things they overlooked, or didn't think were important." He realized this sounded critical of the police, and added, "It's perfectly possible that I wouldn't find anything different or extra at all. But I'd like to try to help if it's all right with you."

She was about to answer when he continued, "I have to ask, in a kind of formal way, because if I have your authorization to represent you it will give me a right to be in certain places. It would be like I was a private detective working on your behalf, although without payment, of course. I couldn't accept payment even if you wanted to pay me because of the licensing laws for private detectives."

Boo said, "You want to investigate Dad's death and you need my permission."

"That's right."

"O.K. You have it."

Willy smiled. "Well, good. So could you make it formal and sign this authorization?" He took out a sheet of paper he had prepared and pushed it her way to read while he looked for a pen.

She didn't take it at first. "I don't really like signing things much."

He wasn't watching while she said it and it wasn't until he found his pen that he saw that it was not a passing comment but a suggestion that she might not sign.

"It's perfectly all right," he said impulsively. Sensed it sounded like a salesman, hard-sell, cliché. "Really, it's just so that if anyone asks me I can show it to them so they don't have to track you down to confirm my authority." She was still uneasy. "Look at it, it's perfectly simple. And you can revoke it at any time."

"O.K., O.K.," she said. And signed.

"And I just hope I can help," he said, returning the document to his jacket pocket.

"Help what?"

"Help find out what happened to your father. Maybe even catch whoever did it." Willy was swept up by having the paper in his pocket.

"Is that all now?"

"Yes, yes." He rose, as did she. "I may well need to ask you some questions sometime, Boo."

"Me?"

"But not now, since it isn't convenient."

"Why me? What kind of questions?"

"About your father, things that I can't find out easily elsewhere. But we'll see how it goes, shall we?" His mood swept down again, listening to himself, the shyster P.I. following ambulances.

"O.K., yeah," she said. She hadn't smiled since they got to the living room.

Willy didn't say anything more until he was outside. He turned back saying, "Have a good time," but the door was already mostly closed and he couldn't see her.

When he entered the house, he thought Nan wasn't there. Which couldn't be right because her car was in the garage. But she didn't feel there.

He gave his head a shake, which passed a shiver through his shoulders the entire length of his spine. He jumped a little. What was he thinking? Why wasn't his mind clear?

He walked through to the living room and found Nan writing a letter. He coughed. She didn't look up.

"I thought you were out," he said.

Without interrupting her writing she said, "Why should you think that?"

"I guess because I didn't hear anything. Not you moving,

or playing the piano or listening to the radio or playing any records."

"Are you telling me I'm generally a noisy person?"

"No," Willy said humbly. He felt humble. He hadn't lived over fifty years to get himself into situations that made him doubt his judgment or feel vulnerable to criticism from his wife. But he felt both.

"Hell," he said, and he sat down.

"Have a good time?" Nan asked formally. She wrote the valedictory comment and signed her name to the letter.

"I didn't go out to have a good time," Willy snapped. After the remark was out, he knew he'd overreacted, that her remark had been an acid prod, paying him back for leaving before dinner.

"No?" she asked archly and artificially, since he'd fallen into her trap. "Business? No, no, don't tell me . . . research! It must have been research." She addressed an envelope.

Willy didn't say anything.

Unexpectedly he felt lighter. It was research. It was his instinct for some unspecified future writing that was driving him in this matter, making him intrude on Hearns, Boo Brinker and others to come.

Nan walked through to the kitchen, where the rack for outgoing letters was, next to the kitchen door. A moment later, she was back in the living room doorway with her hands on her hips. "I've put the food in the oven. Even though you didn't have the decency to tell me when you expected to return home. Are you going to eat with me or did you heap the final insult on my cooking by catching a Big Mac?"

Gratefully Willy walked to the kitchen.

16

"You dumb broad," I said. "That's what you get for not asking questions when Americans pay you to do something."

She looked strikingly beautiful holding her bleeding lip, but I couldn't care less. "My client's wife has just been murdered, by someone who enjoyed it. What do you know about it?"

"Murdered?"

I got in the car. I was in the driver's seat. I took her by the shoulders. "You tell me what you know about it or I'll hang you by your nose on the streetlight in front of the police station."

"I don't know anything about it." She didn't cry; she looked me straight in the eyes. I believed her.

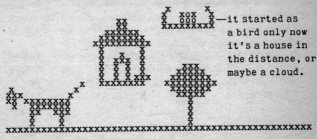

—it started as a bird only now it's a house in the distance, or maybe a cloud.

"Well, in that case we better go see someone who does."

CHAPTER XXIII

17

"You were up there longer today," Nan said. It was by way of a tentative compliment.

"I didn't disturb your midmorning nap with the sound of pounding typewriter keys, did I?"

"What midmorning nap?"

"The one you never take."

"Whatever are you talking about?"

He smiled idiotically. "I dunno."

"Was it all right?"

"What? Oh, the work?" He thought about it. "Sleep helps. I didn't do that much, but at least the quality's back. It's just I've kind of forgotten what's supposed to happen next."

"Do you want to tell me about it?"

"I don't understand it."

"I mean tell me about what is supposed to happen next."

"Oh. No, I don't want to talk it through. I've got some notes somewhere. I'll piece it all together. One of these years. You can read it when it's published."

Nan said nothing.

"I embarked on an old trick at the end."

"Oh yes?"

"Suspense."

"Mmm?"

"I decided to forget what I'd forgotten—most of the stuff in England—and hustle on to the end. So I used a hanging ending and cut the chapter short. That may be the answer. Cut all the chapters short and get them to print it in a bigger typeface than usual."

"How is it really?"

"Really? Really? Really it's great. It's just the words on the pages that aren't coming out so hot. But never fear, Nan my love, never fear. I'll Hank it out in the end. I always have."

"I know," she said. "And if you don't I can always go back to work."

"A low blow, my dear, a low blow indeed."

"You haven't been drinking, have you?"

This shocked him. "I consider that an offensive suggestion."

"It just sounds it, that's all."

"You are not very appreciative. I come down trying to lighten the load of misery I have been laying on you the last few days and all the thanks I get is accusations of dipsomania."

"Did you not sleep well?"

"I slept just fine."

"Really?"

"Really I slept perfectly, except for the part about being unconscious. Otherwise, I slept up a storm."

"I should leave you alone when you're like this. I ought to know that by now."

"No, absolutely no!" Willy said. "Not constructive at all. Because I shall leave you alone instead."

"Oh?"

"Yeah. I'm out now for a bit."

Nan said nothing, loudly.

"On business," Willy said pointedly. And left.

Willy felt unaccustomedly nervous as he stood in the phone booth. The phone rang only twice before it was answered.

"Yeah?"

"Hello, Boo. It is Boo, isn't it?"

"Yeah, who's that?"

"This is Willy Werth."

"Oh, hi, Mr. Werth."

"I was wondering, Boo, about what we talked about last night—you know, I mentioned, I think, that I was going to want to ask you a couple of questions."

"Again?"

"I mentioned it, I'm sure."

"I guess so, yeah."

"And I wondered if it would be convenient sometime today. I don't want to put you out, but if I'm going to get anywhere I'm going to have to know more than I do about your father."

"Gee, this sounds just like the movies."

In a moment of irritation Willy said, "Movies can be a lot like real life. Is there sometime today that would be all right?"

Boo thought about it. "Yeah, you can come out, only I was just going over to the Lido to play tennis, and after that I . . ." She thought again.

"You play a lot of tennis?"

"Not much else to do in Indianapolis," she said. "And I don't know whether I'm coming home again after that. Could I talk to you at the Lido? Would that be good enough? I don't have a fixed game but I said that I would be there. There's this guy I was just nuts over in high school that didn't like me and I'm going to show him what he missed."

Willy said, "Yes, I can come over to the tennis club."

"How long is it going to take?"

"It shouldn't take long. Half an hour, maybe, to give me enough to get me started. Where shall we meet?"

"How 'bout the fruit-vending machine?"

"The—?"

"Oh, don't you know it?" Boo asked. "It drove me crazy when I saw it. It's so wholesome! It's this machine with refrigerated fruit inside the main entrance. Apples and oranges and stuff."

"I'll find it," Willy said.

Willy was at the Lido in twelve minutes and waited only two before Boo walked in.

"I didn't expect you so soon," he said.

"What's the matter, your girl friends always late?"

"No," he said reflectively. "Must just be my cultural upbringing."

"You found my fruity O.K. then, huh?"

"No problem."

"Those would do a bomb in New York, they really would. They're crazy about country stuff there, those city people. I had this idea to rent some space and bring some cows in and charge people to milk them. They'd go wild!"

"The people or the cows?"—

"You don't think it's such a good idea? Well, I do. Where should we go?"

"I don't know," Willy said. "I've been here to go swimming, but not for anything else, so I don't know the layout."

"There's a cafeteria looking over the courts. I don't know if the bar is open this early. You want a drink?"

With a small smile, Willy said, "Not while I'm working."

Boo led him to the cafeteria and suddenly Willy began to feel nervous. Out of his element began to confuse in his mind

with out of his league. She sat at a picnic-style bench next to
a window that overlooked the tennis courts. She studied the
players carefully, then turned back to Willy. He was standing,
looking at her.

"Something wrong?" she asked.

"No." He slid in across the table from her. "You are really
spectacularly pretty."

"Yeah, I know." She glanced at the courts again. Then
seemed to remember that she had already examined them. "I
made a movie, once."

"But I don't think it played here."

Unexpectedly she giggled. "I don't think it 'played' hardly
anywhere."

"No?"

"Not with ads in the papers and a hometown premiere. It
wasn't that kind of movie."

"So I understand."

She looked at his eyes for a moment. "Would you like to
see it?"

"Mightn't it increase my risk from coronaries?"

"I could lend you my print," she said. "I've got a print, see.
I didn't get much money but they gave me a copy and that's
not cheap, you know."

Willy nodded.

"And I thought it would be nice to have a copy, for when
I'm older and...different."

"A long time from now," Willy said, attempting to recoup
by flattery.

"Who told you about my movie?" she asked.

"You did. But your father mentioned it, too."

Boo nodded slowly. "I kinda thought he didn't really think
it was a disaster like he told me he thought."

Willy said, "I want to ask you some things about your
father."

"On the way over I was thinking that I don't really know
that much about him. When I was a kid, he was pretty nice
to me. Specially when I was in high school." She waved toward
the courts. "We played a lot of tennis, for instance."

"Are you good?"

"I'm pretty good for a looker," she said, then suddenly
giggled. "I nearly said, 'for a hooker.'"

The giggle was slightly infectious and Willy felt himself
smile more than he felt.

Boo slapped her mouth, sharply. "Naughty mouth, naughty." She looked away to the tennis courts. "And he was really nice when I was a little kid, but that's not what you want to know about, is it?"

"I guess not."

"Well, shoot away."

Willy concentrated. "Thing is, the key to a crime like this is to work out why it was committed. Once you have an idea why, it's far easier to get an idea of who."

"That policeman said it would probably end up some looney."

"To say it's a looney just means he can't explain it. It doesn't mean it isn't explainable." Willy grew more comfortable, in an area of his established opinionatedness. "I'd like to know more about how your father passed his time. Let's take the business."

"I don't know much about that."

"Well, I've been to the site and seen some of the trailers. But did he do any other kind of business?"

Boo looked puzzled.

"I write books, for instance," Willy said. "But I also get invited to talk to groups or be on panels or things that aren't actually writing at all. I just wondered if your father spent time doing other things or whether he was at West Washington all day."

"I don't know. I've been away these two years, see."

"Without coming home at all?"

"I kind of left under difficult circumstances."

"Oh, I didn't know."

"I ran away," Boo said. "With an older man. I thought it was going to last forever, but it only lasted six weeks. Only, by the end that kind of seemed forever."

"Ah," Willy said.

"That guy at work, the guy who's kind of taken things over there, he could tell you more about Dad recently than I could."

"I talked to him a bit the other day, but I'll see him again."

"I've never met him but he has a dreamy voice on the phone."

"O.K.," Willy said. "But now could you think about your father's private life?"

Boo looked a little shocked.

"I mean the part of his life that wasn't business. Personal friends, tastes, hobbies."

"He still played tennis and some squash. That what you mean?"

"Did he play here?"

"The tennis. I think he did the squash downtown at the Athletic Club."

"O.K.," Willy said.

"And there was all that old furniture."

"The antiques. Where and when did he acquire most of those?"

"God, I don't know. Auctions, sometimes, I think. But you know you really ought to ask Mom this kind of stuff."

Willy instinctively withdrew from the notion. Too indelicate. "There's some sense to that, of course. But it doesn't really seem right for an outsider to pry."

"The cop didn't seem to mind."

"It's different if it's your job. I'm only a volunteer," Willy said. "But maybe you could ask your mother about your father's routines, who he saw, that kind of thing..."

"Oooo, I don't know. We don't talk much, you know."

"It would be very helpful. Of great assistance."

"Well."

"And a look through his papers. If he had a desk at home, some of the things that he kept in it might be useful. When you get a chance."

"Well, I'll think about it."

Willy was understanding. "I know the idea of going through your father's things must be hard."

But Boo was confused for a moment. "You mean 'cause he's dead and all? That wasn't what I was thinking about. No, it's just I'm kinda keeping pretty busy and I don't know if I'm going to get a chance, leastways not when Mom isn't breathing over my shoulder."

"Oh."

"I get in trouble if I stick around the house a lot. She's always getting at me. So I try to get out as much as I can, see."

"Well, it must be a difficult time for you both."

"What time is it, Mr. Werth?"

Willy showed her.

"Can I go now? I want to work up my full you-caught-me-off-guard casual effect."

"All right. But I will need to ask you some more things later, Boo."

"That's O.K., Mr. Werth. Sorry to dash off like this. It's just I like to be on time when I get a time in mind. It makes me different."

She disappeared in the direction of the lobby.

Willy stared after her and then was hit by a wave of self-consciousness. He wondered what he was doing. He pursed his lips, and turned to watch the tennis courts for a minute.

The tennis-court reservation clerk was housed in a small booth near the entrance to the courts. Willy found him seated behind the registration counter with his eyes closed. He was a gaunt pockmarked old man and Willy wondered whether he was dead.

He wasn't. Before Willy spoke, the man said, "Nothing left for today."

"What?"

The man looked at Willy. "Are you a new member or an invited guest, or what? I don't recognize you, do I?"

"I don't suppose you do. But I don't want to book a court."

"No? What then?"

Willy took a breath. "I need some information."

The man wiggled his ears. "I don't know much."

"About someone who played here regularly."

"Oh yeah?" the man said, without overwhelming interest.

"Brinker. Larry . . . Lawrence Brinker."

"Brinker, Brinker, Brinker, Brinker, Brinker," the man said.

"Yes."

"Most Wednesday afternoons."

"He played Wednesday afternoons?"

"That's right. He missed a booking yesterday. We held it ten minutes, then let it go."

"He was killed Sunday night," Willy said.

"You don't say. Well, they come and they go."

"Do you remember him?"

The man thought. "Little mustache?"

"Yes."

"Bit shorter than you, more muscles?"

"If you want to put it that way, I guess so."

"Yeah, I recollect him."

"What I wanted to know," Willy said, "was whether he had

any regular partners. Someone he played with regularly or often."

"You mean the tall boy?"

"I guess so."

"A guest. Mr. Brinker signed him in."

"Do you know his name?"

"No. But it will be in the book."

"Could you look it up for me, please?"

The man shrugged, leafed back a week and found the name. "A. Smith."

Willy wrote it down. "You don't know his address, do you?"

"Nope," the man said, but there was a curiosity in his expression. "Looking for a tennis partner like that young fella, huh?"

"Like what?" Willy asked.

"Oh, nothing," the man said.

"Young, you mean? Or tall?" The man shook his head. "Well, what?"

"Nothing, really," the man said. "Just he was kind of delicate for tennis. Delicate."

"Delicate?"

"If you know what I mean."

"So you're not a cop?"

"I never said I was," Willy said. He took his authorizing letter and put it back in his pocket.

"You sure lorded it around like a cop," Barry Youngman said. But he was more irritated than hostile.

"I didn't worry you, did I?"

"Me? Naw, I don't worry. You get to my age"—he looked at Willy—"our age, you can't spend time worrying."

"I've got a few more questions," Willy said.

"So what do you want to know?" Youngman leaned back in his chair behind the desk.

Willy stopped before he started. "Are you alone again today?"

"Yeah. Shifty's sick. I thought he was faking it at first, but it's some jazz with his spleen or liver or something."

"What's his address?" Willy asked.

Youngman hesitated but said, "He's got an apartment in

Lynhurst, towards town." He looked up the street and number
and wrote it out for Willy. "You going to see him?"

"Probably. Why?"

"No reason," Youngman mused. "He says he'll have a doctor's note when he comes. Not that it matters much. We haven't
sold anything all week."

"Is this usually a busy time of year?"

"It's getting to the end of the season, but it's never this bad.
We shift from R.V.s to trailer-park stuff about now. But we're
not even getting tourists asking directions. They must think
murder is catching."

Willy said with gravity, "Murder isn't a random kind of
thing."

"What's that supposed to mean?"

"It means people are killed for reasons. And what I want
to find out first is why Mr. Brinker was killed."

"That I can't tell you," Youngman said. He ran fingers back
through his waved white hair.

"I didn't say you could."

"I thought you were asking."

"Something you can tell me is why Mr. Brinker was in the
trailer he was killed in."

"He used to do his late paperwork there."

"Why not here?"

"I don't know," Youngman said. "He could have. He said
it was small and it certainly isn't as comfortable as the trailer."

"Did he do a lot of after-hours paperwork?"

"I wouldn't have said a lot. Of course, I wasn't around to
keep tabs on him."

"You figure his use of the trailer might have been more
social than business?" Willy asked.

"A bit of snatch?" Youngman smiled and shrugged. "Well,
I never saw any."

"What sort of thing did Mr. Brinker do regularly?" Willy
asked. "When was he here?"

"Well, he was here more often than not. Except he was
away most Monday and Friday mornings and Wednesday afternoons."

"What did he do?"

"He had people he saw."

"Business people?"

"Yeah, I guess so."

"Did he come back with orders or bills or other business papers?"

"I don't know. Sometimes."

"So it might not have been business?"

"I don't know what it was. He was the boss. He was screwing his wife, for all I know. It wasn't up to me to ask."

"If it was business, what might it have been?"

"Well . . ." Youngman gave it some thought. "There are various contract buyers. Like for building-site offices or the state. He was also thinking hard about moving into pre-fab stuff. Without wheels, I mean. And there are the trailer-park people, problems with units we've sold, all that sort of thing. It's a pretty competitive business, and you've got to keep your finger on it all the time. He might have been scouting the opposition or seeing reps from trailer companies, or the repairers or the delivery agency. There's plenty to do."

"Delivery agency?"

"If we got an order that was too far for us to deliver easily, or wasn't convenient. Within the state we do it ourselves. The Kid did a lot."

"The Kid? Oh yeah, he was your other salesman."

"Well, not a salesman quite. He did a lot of the pickup and delivery kind of work. The errands, you know."

"And where's he today?"

"He quit."

"When?"

"Yesterday. Well, you can't blame him. Things have been completely fucked up. Nobody knows if they're going to be here tomorrow or not, do they? Not really."

"So why haven't you quit?"

"Two reasons."

"Yes?" Willy waited for them.

"I'm too old to be impatient."

"Yeah?"

A bit of a smile: "And I called Brinker's daughter. She wants me to take charge, at least for the time being. So I'm keeping busy." Pointedly, "Even when I don't have people coming in asking me questions."

"I see."

"Call me insensitive," Youngman said, "but it's an ill wind. If I do good and Mrs. Brinker decides to keep the business going, maybe I'll be kept as manager. I'm not counting on anything, but it's to nobody's advantage if I let things get run down: So I'm fixing the bell for the telephone and keeping the ads going into the paper. All that kinda stuff."

"Where were you on the night of the murder?" Willy asked.

"What?"

"Where were you?"

"You have a goddam nerve. I was at home, that's where."

"Your wife will back that up?"

"I'm not married anymore."

The telephone rang. Youngman stared at Willy for a moment before answering it. Willy waited while the caller heard that Larry Brinker had passed away unexpectedly, but they were conducting business as usual.

"You've got to tell them that or you'll lose them," Youngman said to Willy.

"You've been in this business quite awhile?"

Youngman nodded.

"Been around?"

"A bit."

"Ever tried to go it on your own?"

"Once or twice."

"Or three times?"

"Twice, if you count the time with a partner. The first winter is the ball-breaker. If you can get through that first winter, you're all right."

"But you didn't get through it?"

Youngman shrugged, as if the forgotten yoke of his business failures had come back with retrospective weight.

"There was something you said the other day, about that argument Mr. Brinker had."

"With the hippie type? About his trailer?"

"That's it."

"I told you—and the police—you're wasting your time there."

"I don't remember asking your opinion about it," Willy said. "Did you notice the license plate on his car on the guy's trailer?"

"I didn't take the number down," Youngman said sharply.

"What kind of trailer was it?" Willy asked.

"A model called a Tow-EZ. It's a small vacation camper type. This was about six years old, pretty well fitted out and in good condition except it was covered in spray decorations."

"Decorations?"

"Kind of artwork, you know. Only nothing lewd like some of them."

"What did Mr. Brinker offer for it?"

"Two hundred and thirty-five dollars."

"How much would a similar one cost new?"

"About twenty-two hundred."

Willy raised his eyebrows. "What would the resale be?"

"Maybe seven hundred. Or four fifty-four eighty elsewhere in the trade. But we'd have had it resprayed first. No, the guy said he was in a hurry. And it was Mr. Brinker's first offer. We might have gone a little over three hundred if the guy had played the game. But he went off half cocked instead, so Mr. Brinker told him to get out."

"And did he?"

"Sure. After sounding off a little. But honest, it was nothing special. The kind of thing happens a lot."

"Only not that particular week."

"No."

"On the night of the murder, you say you were at home."

Youngman said nothing.

"Were you alone?"

"I had nothing to do with the murder of Mr. Brinker," he said, "and if you ask me questions like I did, I'll bust you one."

"I don't think that will be necessary," Willy said. "At the moment."

Lynhurst was only a few minutes from Brinker's Mobile Homes, an ill-defined aluminum district extending from part of West Washington Street to the north.

The address turned out to be a former motel.

Willy couldn't make out what it had been called. The fifteen-foot sign had long since been smashed into a spatula-shaped metal monument to former glories.

Willy parked outside and walked into the drive-in courtyard.

There were two cars and no people. The stucco front walls of the former motel rooms were chipping and the paint bubbled on the door and window frames.

The only unit clearly numbered matched the number Willy had been given for Shifty.

Willy knocked at the door.

After a minute, it opened slowly.

"Mr. Shilton?"

"Who wants him?"

Willy couldn't see clearly into the room, but said, "It's a little complicated, but I represent the Brinker family."

The door opened to reveal a short man of about thirty with bad teeth and ruddy pink cheeks. "That's O.K. then," he said. "You get some funny people around here, Born Again Christians, door-to-door pimps, all sorts. If you're straight, you gotta be careful."

Willy walked into the room. It was immaculate, organized and a total contrast to the world outside the door.

"I was just doing my ironing," Shifty said. "One day I'm gonna make someone a wonderful wife."

Willy sat on the edge of a cushioned chair while Shilton hung three shirts in a closet that seemed full to bursting with clothes.

"Hey, you're not checking on me being sick, are you?" Shifty said, sitting on the bed across from Willy. "I told Hairy Barry I'd bring in a verification from the doc when I came, and I will."

"No," Willy said.

"Oh. You're here to fire me."

"No," Willy said.

Shilton bounced back on the bed. "That's a relief. I was afraid they were going to close the place down." He sat up again.

"I don't know what the plans for the business are."

"Well, what can I do you for? Not looking for a trailer on the side cheap, are you? That's not my scene. I'm the straight one, remember? The guy who is trying to make something of himself by working his way through college."

"I didn't know that," Willy said.

"Well, who the hell are you?" Shilton asked in a friendly way.

"I'm getting details and background for the family about what happened to Mr. Brinker."

"I don't know anything about it, except what I read in the paper."

"You were in on Tuesday," Willy said, "the day Mr. Brinker was found."

"I spent most of the day in the john. I was throwing up all the time."

"What is wrong with you?"

"I get these kinds of fits," Shilton said. "I don't know a lot about it, only I went in for tests and they say I shouldn't walk around much. I feel O.K. now, but in an hour maybe I won't be able to stand up."

"That must be pretty worrying for you."

"Naw, I don't worry. They say not to worry, so I don't. I've never been a worrier since my wife split with me. I used to drink heavy but now I pulled myself together. I held the job with Brinker for five years. Doing O.K. and going to college nights. I'm going to be rich and famous and somebody. So why should I worry?"

"Have you got any idea why anyone would want to kill Mr. Brinker?" Willy asked.

"No," Shifty said. "It was a fuckall shock."

"No business enemies?"

"Nobody's a friend in this business, but people don't go around with machine guns."

"Any idea of private activities that might have got him in trouble?"

"Like what?"

Willy smiled. "I don't know what his private activities were."

"Well, I only saw him at work," Shilton said, spreading his hands to draw attention to the one-room home he filled so completely. "Never really felt like inviting him over for socializing. I'm cutting all the corners till I graduate. After I'd made it, then maybe I would have got to know him better privately. Man to man, equal to equal, you know?"

"Did Mr. Brinker do you any favors to help you along?"

"What favors? I do my job. I do it good enough. Who's doing who the favor?"

"What were you doing Sunday night?" Willy asked.

"Sitting on the can doing my homework."

"What amazes me," Willy said, "is how easy it is." Excitement bubbled through voice and body.

Nan served him a bowl of reheated soup.

"I just ask these guys questions and they answer me. I thought I was going to have to struggle just to get a civil reaction or two, but the real problem was thinking out what to ask next. I wasn't prepared with a list of things I wanted to know, but I felt they'd have told me their grandmother's eye color if I'd put the question."

"Most people are ready enough to talk about themselves," Nan said. "Especially to someone who isn't threatening."

"Like a real policeman, you mean?" Willy asked. "Maybe you're right, maybe you're right. But it's still exhilarating. Imagine, complete strangers opening up to you like that. I tell you, it's enough to make me believe in private detectives."

"Didn't you before?" she asked. But he was paying little attention.

"And another thing that exhilarated me even more is the sense that I may end up doing some good. I may come across something that will really help. That's a charge, that is."

"Your soup will get cold."

"It's a matter of motive," Willy said. "In books, I've always stressed how important motive is. And I wouldn't be surprised if the police tend to forget that sometimes. I'm hardly at the heart of the case but I haven't heard anyone even speculate yet about why Larry was killed."

"Look, do you want that soup or not?" Nan asked.

"I want it, I want it."

"It's getting colder the more you talk. If you don't want it, I'll pour it away."

"I was just trying to make you feel how exciting these sessions with the guys from Brinker's were."

"I'd be more interested if you were telling me about how Hank was bullying suspects instead of how you were bullying suspects."

"They both seemed pretty convincing about not being involved," Willy said. "But if you come down to it, neither has what you could call a real alibi. Not on what they said."

"Just how much time do you intend to spend solving Larry Brinker's murder?"

Willy had turned to his soup. His face showed it was too cold. But he said, "This thing has really got my blood moving around, you know?"

"What are you going to do about your deadline?"

"Have them put it back if I have to," he said.

"It throws out their production schedule, doesn't it?"

"Other people miss deadlines occasionally, for good reasons. Stop nagging me."

Nan stopped. One of Willy's points of pride was his punctuality with his work. His abandonment of the principle underlined how serious the diversion had become.

"I'm allowed a little artistic temperament now and then."

"I didn't say anything."

"I could hear you thinking." More soup. "I'm not losing that much time from work."

"Yet."

"We'll worry about it when it happens."

"But even when you do work, it isn't going very well."

"How do you know?"

"You said so."

"Did I? I've got to learn to keep my mouth shut, don't I?" He pushed his empty bowl across the table to her and she took it, with hers, to the sink.

"If he was a real friend, I think I'd understand it better."

"He was more than an acquaintance. Besides, it's not the sort of thing that happens every day."

"I'm not going to complain about it any more, Willy. I'm going to try not to. But I don't feel I understand, and that makes me . . . uncertain."

The telephone rang.

They looked at each other for a moment. They both moved to answer the call. Each, seeing the other moving, stopped. Then Nan picked up the receiver.

"Hello?"

"Hi, this is Boo Brinker. Is Willy there?"

Nan held the receiver away from her ear. Without covering the mouthpiece: "A 'Boo Brinker' asking for 'Willy.' I think it's for you, Mr. Werth."

Unable to do anything else, Willy took the phone. "Hello." Nan watched him thoughtfully.

"Hi. This is Boo. What I'm calling about is I was wondering if you could come over to our place now."

"Now?" Willy asked. Self-consciously he glanced at Nan.

"If you can. It's pretty important."

"Yes, I can. I'll be there in about half an hour."

"Great," Boo said. "Bye."

Nan watched without speaking as Willy hung up.

"I'll work later," Willy said, abruptly defensive. "Like I ordinarily do when I have something to do in the afternoon."

"Well, well, well," Nan said. "I've long held the opinion

that a girl would have to be crazy to go for an egomaniac like
Hank Midwinter. But I always was discriminating. And maybe
a lot of people aren't."

The door was answered by Lorraine Brinker.

"Oh!" Willy was flustered. "Is . . . uh. Boo called and asked
me to come out. Is she here?"

"She called you for me, Willy."

"For you?"

"Come in. Come in. Do come in."

Willy was led to the living room and guided to a well-worn
and very comfortable leather wing chair.

"That was Larry's favorite," Lorraine said, with a sad smile.
"Is it comfortable? Do you like it?" Tears came to her eyes as
she stood in front of man and chair.

"It's very nice," Willy said.

"Oh, I am glad you like it." She rubbed her eyes. "Can I
get you anything?" she asked. "Some beer. Please let me get
you something."

"O.K.," Willy said. "A beer."

Almost running, Lorraine disappeared from the room.

Willy stood up. He went to the hall to look for signs of
Boo. He thought about leaving. He looked out the window.

Lorraine Brinker returned carrying a large glass of beer and
an unopened can. "Oh!" she said, seeing him at the window.
"You don't like the chair after all."

"I do," Willy said. "I was just looking at . . . things. . . ." He
turned back to the room. "There are some lovely antiques here."

Instead of saying anything, Lorraine set the beer containers
on the nearest surface and wiped her eyes again. She turned
away.

Shocked, Willy took the glass and can off the polished
tabletop. It was not meant for cold beer.

Now holding both containers, he said, "Uh, which one is
yours?" He held out the glass.

He stood there for a long time. Lorraine Brinker dried her
tears and then cried some more. Finally she took the glass and
sipped from it. "Just a little," she said. "It's really yours, but
I'll just have a sip."

She drank half, quickly, and handed it back to Willy with

heavy lipstick marks remaining on the rim. She sat down on the couch near the leather armchair.

Willy took his place again. There was a silence, which made him uneasy, so he said, "You said that Boo called me for you."

"I don't know what to do about her, Willy, I really don't."

Willy wasn't prepared for the comment. His attention had been drawn to the bright way Lorraine Brinker's eyes shone from above the dark, dark bags under them.

"Don't feel you have to be tactful about her," Lorraine said.

"I don't know that I feel I am entitled to make any kind of judgment about her."

"You're being a good friend to me, Willy, the way you've offered to help about Larry." Lorraine snuffled briefly, but only briefly. "You're being a really good friend." She put a hand around Willy's hand as he held the can of beer. She pressed hard and held her hand there for a long time. She said, "Boo's such a flibbertigibbet. I think it's her attitude more than anything. I mean, she's out playing tennis now. With her father not buried yet. I mean, tennis! Not that I want her sitting around crying all the time, Willy. I'm not like that. We have to come to grips with the fact that we're alive and that life is for the living. But what Larry would say, with her prancing around in her . . . her tennis things. I mean, it's not much more than underwear, is it, Willy? Tell me honestly, now, is it much more than her underwear?" Lorraine looked unswervingly into Willy's face.

Willy said, "Well."

She took her hand away to wipe her nose. Willy finished the glass of beer and found a glass-topped table for the tumbler and the can. He turned back to her with his hands at his sides.

She waited for his answer.

Willy said, "But she has taken on a number of responsibilities, because of the circumstances." No response. "And she came back home immediately."

"What else should she do?"

"She's doing what she should do," Willy said. "That's my point."

"Since she left home, Willy," Lorraine Brinker edged forward, "Boo has just gone to pot. To pot! And I mean that literally, too. While she was here, she was a good clean popular girl. But some of the stories she tells about New York! My

God, I couldn't repeat them, and she just laughs. Things people
do there. And it's not just the movie she was in. That was a
bit of fun for her and you can't blame her for having looks and
taking the opportunity to use them a little. Movies are all acting,
anyway, aren't they? Things look real and you can't see how
they couldn't be real but they aren't real. That's just the way
in movies, isn't it? But it's things she tells me that aren't in
the movies. It's horrible to say it, but I'm almost thankful that
Larry isn't here to listen to her talk about how some of the
people she knows carry on. His little girl. His little girl!"

Suddenly Lorraine stopped. She hid her face in her hands
and shook. But there were no cries, no tears, and taking a deep
breath she dropped her hands and looked at Willy again.

"There, see? I'm under control."

"I'm just sorry there's nothing I can do to help," Willy said,
feeling deeply that it was said lamely.

"But you are helping," Lorraine said hotly. "You are! It's
so good of you to find out who did it. I'm sure you will, too.
And I'm sure that you dealing with Boo is good for her, too.
Some of the older men she's got involved with—oh goodness,
I just won't tell you the things they would have had her up to
if she didn't have at least a little spark of decency and common
sense. Though why she should always get involved with the
old fogeys, I can't understand. The boys her age are so cute
now."

Willy drank some beer.

"Willy," she said suddenly, "the funeral is tomorrow afternoon. Would you say a few words? About Larry, maybe some
things that would be good advice for young people like Boo.
Would you do that for me?"

"Uh. Well."

"For me," Lorraine said. She pushed her tired face to what
had been coquettish when she was young.

"It's not that I wouldn't want to," Willy said, "but I—I
don't think I could."

"Don't be modest! Being a writer, I'm sure you would do
it beautifully."

"But I didn't know Larry that well."

"I can tell you anything you need to know," Lorraine Brinker
said with enthusiasm. "If anybody should know about Larry,
I should."

"But it's not the sort of thing that someone outside the family should do. There must be a relative. Someone . . ."

Lorraine Brinker sat down on the couch. "Arthur can do it, I suppose. I just thought—I thought you might want to do it. With all the interest you're showing in me."

"Who is Arthur?"

"Why, Larry's brother."

"He would be more appropriate, really, don't you think?"

"If you don't want to, just say so."

"It's not that."

"If you think I'm not capable of making reasonable decisions . . . That's what Boo says and she does what she likes no matter what I feel."

"You seem capable of making reasonable decisions to me," Willy said.

Lorraine Brinker smiled and nodded. "You are nice," she said. "You are trying and that's wonderful."

Willy wasn't certain what she was referring to.

"I took a call for Boo from Barry Youngman at the site, and he told me you're taking time to help. And I do appreciate it, William, I really do. And I can prove it." She stood up again and ran out of the room.

She had a paper in her hand when she returned. "I had this made for you," she said. He took it, and she said, "It's a copy of Larry's death certificate. I thought you might want it."

Willy studied the sheet.

"See?" she said. "It has the results of the autopsy and everything. Cause of death, time of death, all that sort of thing. That's a help, isn't it? Isn't it?"

"Oh, yes," Willy forced himself to say. "It could be."

"Oh," she said. There was some disappointment.

"It should be, really," Willy said. "Bound to be."

"It wasn't easy to get," Lorraine said. "Ordinarily they don't send two copies, not even to the next of kin. But I insisted."

"Well," Willy said. "I'm very grateful."

"That's really what I asked you to come out for," she said.

It was a moment before Willy realized she was suggesting that he should leave.

Swamped by a sense of confusion that seemed to come from the lack of an alternative, Willy made his way home to work. Awash in the waves of his investigation, he hardly felt like it.

But he had said he would work later, and he was driving toward making good his word in body, if not in spirit.

Nan was sitting at the kitchen table poring over account books. She smiled as he came and said, "No need to work! I've just found a mistake in the bank statement which gives us an extra three dollars and fourteen cents!"

"Oh yes?" Willy said.

"Come on," she said, "I wasn't getting at you."

"I believe you," Willy said. "But I always was gullible." He went upstairs.

18

Writer's block is a very fine thing, the kind of phenomenon fit for a king, the kind of life story that lyricists sing, something something whatsit with a bee's-tail sting.

Come come, now, William. This isn't real writer's block. Block is wanting to and not being able to. You don't want to.

People like the Terre Haute Writers' Circle are going to ask you whether you only write when you're in the mood or whether you have to force yourself. And you're going to tell them that you only write when you're in the mood but you're in the mood regularly twice a day.

They are going to chortle and cheer and none of them is going to know that you pinched the principle from Willy Faulkner. So you will pass for a wit in their circle. Circle! Hah.

But when you're not in the mood...

Christ, what do you do? Must be a block. I mean it is A Block even if not The Block.

Oh dear, oh dear. It's just as well for me to have some time up here tinkling the typewriter, fiddling its diddle so Nan can hear work being done from above. Not that she really intrudes, to the extent of standing behind and watching the production line over my shoulder. But she's a foreman, for all that.

Tell me, sir, now that you've stopped, how did you get started writing?

Well, Madam...there I was in the army with mud on my hands and I thought there must be something else I can do than dig ditches. And that's how I started writing.

How fascinating, Mr. Werth, could it really have happened like that?

No, it couldn't, Madam. Only sometimes I think digging ditches would be more satisfying.

How could that be, Mr. Werth?

Why, after a week's digging ditches you end up with a guaranteed ditch, Madam. If I work for a week, I may end up with a moment of lucidity and I realize I should have been writing it another way. So I have to throw it away and all I have left is the backs of the sheets of paper to take telephone messages on.

Oh.

God, how boring it's going to be. Yes, I write under my own name. No, I am not Hank.

No, let's correct that. It's not going to be boring. I am going to be boring.

Do you really throw it all away, Mr. Werth? Really?

Nope. Never. I scavenge. There are always good bits in a week's work. I cut 'em out and put them in the rewrites whenever I can.

Cut them out? With scissors, you mean?

Certainly not with brothers.

I wish I had a beer.

Do you often drink beer when you work, Mr. Werth? Or use other stimulants?

Beer isn't a stimulant, Madam.

But do—?
No, never.
But you just asked for a beer.
Ah, but I'm not working, Madam.

Mind you, I suppose, if I am sitting on my career-
flattened ass up here I might as well think about
what to do with Hank next.

Hank, Hank, Hank, Hank. The name slips nimbly
off the tongue.
What to do with him.
What's been happening to him? Hell, I forget. So I
look it up. Writing is like digging ditches. Once you've
written something, it stays there unless you're
careless with matches. So what was the old bugger
doing when last sighted?
Hell, all I have on the top of my desk is a wretched
certificate of death. Death. Death.
Not Hank's, however. Not yet.
Ah ah ah ah. He's just socked poor old Mossman
after he's found poor old Stella McKeand chopped up.
Um.
Wasn't I going to have him wander around Frome
tracking down that guy Brock Hallett? Um. And go
back to that storefront and do things to the lady he
met there before.
And get chased by police. And get away and come
back to Indy.
Mmmmmmm.
I'm uneasy about this Hank in England stuff. May
have been stretching a bit to get him there.
The idea was all right. To do something different
and challenge and expand my mind and his a bit.
But I didn't expect Brinker.
It would be all right if I were more comfortable
with how things are done in England. But having to
learn it to write about it...

Decision. I will get Hank back to the U.S.
Immediately.

Time lapse, that's it. The old ploy, just have him
appear in the new situation and reveal later how he
got there.

It's like the old serialist's nightmare. In a fit of
creative frenzy you put Captain Miracle in the
clutches of a creature so potent that you can't think
of a way to get him out of the creature-clutches.

So you don't.

You start the next week with his walking into the
office of General Miracle, who says, "That sure was a
close call." Then whisk off to next creature.

So, Hank's next creature...

Woodrow McKeand. Gangster and art collector. Of
Indianapolis.

Damn foreign countries, can't trust 'em. What good
is a country you can't get your Wheaties in, I ask you.

I wonder if they have Wheaties over there....

Perhaps I'll wonder about that in more detail
tomorrow.

Why tomorrow? Is it just that you want beer?

A mad craving for beer...

Well, earn it.

For a change.

CHAPTER XXIII

When the plane landed at Weir Cook Airport, I didn't
bother to go home. I changed my shirt in the men's
room, splashed my face with the coldest water I could
find in an available tap and I got The Doodah out of
hock from the parking lot.

Mossman was with me.

I hadn't exactly kidnapped her, but she was
involved, so I encouraged her by force to see scenic
Indianapolis. Maybe she would like it. There's no
accounting for tastelessness.

But before I could get things moving I had to clear
my mind.

I took the Doodah out for a run on Interstate 465.

Driving at a hundred requires concentration. I did
half an hour north and then twenty-seven minutes
back again.

The Doodah cleared her throat as I cleared my
head, which is why we made better time on the back
nine. She'd clogged up a bit sitting in the lot. Good
Doodahs, like good women, need regular use.

Mossman sat in her seat without opening her face
for the whole hour. The less she talked the more I
liked her. Setting aside the fact that no woman should
take on a job like mine, she wasn't too bad. Maybe in
a place like England where the living is quieter and
where they have to import their throat-slashers from
the States, where the crooks are polite like everybody
else, maybe there she could get along.

As a P.I. in Indianapolis, she'd be murdered before
she had time to starve to death.

But as girl dicks went, she was O.K.

Not that I like private investigators. They're not
nice people.

I certainly had no plans to be nice people.

"Ever been to Indy?" I asked.

"What? Me?"

"Who the hell else do you think I was talking to?"
We were waiting at a red light in the middle of town. I
was thinking of poetry.

"No," she said. "I've never been to America before."

"What do you think of it so far?"

"It's like they say," she said, "life is much faster
here."

"You've got to keep moving or something will get
you from behind."

"Like what?" she asked.

Hell, I don't know. I keep finding my mind coming
back to death certificates.

"Like what happened to Stella McKeand," I said.

"We're off to see about that."

"But what can we do here?"

"We can

19

Nan opened the door to Willy's office. "There's a man downstairs to see you, Willy."

"What the hell are you talking about? Can't you see I'm in midstream?"

"He's a policeman. I said you were not to be disturbed, but he said if I didn't come up to get you, he would do it himself."

Willy turned to her and frowned.

"It's the one from the Brinkers'."

"What the hell does he want?" Willy asked. But it was a rhetorical question. He had already pulled his typewriter's cover over his work.

Hearns stood in the middle of the living room and glared as Willy entered. "You are in trouble," he said with moderate tones that reeked of disciplined hostility.

"What do you—"

"I don't know what kind of game you think you are playing, but I will not tolerate anybody interfering with the course of a murder investigation."

"I'm not inter—"

"You figure you are some kind of privileged character but you have no more rights than any other member of the public. And that means you keep clear of witnesses, you keep clear of scenes of the crime, you keep clear of relatives, you keep clear period."

"I don't think you under—"

"You will not, repeat not, go to Brinker's Mobile Homes and question the salesmen. You will not question anyone. And if I'm not getting through to you, or if you are just stupid, if you keep interfering, then I shall take time from my busy case load and I shall see to it that you are prosecuted for your troubles. Do you understand that?"

"Why don't you give me a chan—"

"Do you *understand*?"

"Of course I understa—"

"You *understand*? Yes or no?"

"Yes, of course I understand the words. But when—"

"All right then. Now I've made my point, I can stop wasting taxpayers' money and get back to work." Hearns strode toward the doorway, where Nan jumped aside.

"But I'm authorized," Willy called after him. "I have—"

Hearns stopped and pivoted to face Willy again. "Authorized?" he asked, rolling the word out as if it had only just been invented, as if he had never heard it before, as if he had only just discerned its meaning. "Is this because you are an author?"

"What? Oh. No. The Brinkers have authorized me to investigate what happened to—"

"The Brinkers? And just who are you to investigate a murder, Mr. Werth? Are you a . . . a marshal of the wild West? Or a C.I.A. spy? Or king of the Martian Military Police? Just what is it you are pretending to be?"

"I'm not pretending. I'm sort of a private investigator for the family. Not to replace the police investigation, let me assure you of that."

"Oh, I am so relieved!" Cement-slab irony. "I can keep my job. Oh, my wife and children will be so happy."

"There's no need to be snide about it."

"And may I see your private investigator's license then?"

"Ah, I don't need one."

"And why would that be?"

"Because I'm not taking money for it. The words of the statute talk about doing investigative work for hire or reward. I'm not. So I don't need a license."

"What are you working for then—love?"

"No, of course not."

"What for then, Mr. Werth?" Hearns's volume began to increase again. "Why exactly are you interfering in this case, Mr. Werth?"

"For a kind of interest. I wouldn't rally expect you to understand. There's an oblig—"

"You're right there, Werth. I don't understand."

Pushed past his limit, Willy shouted back. "I just feel obliged to try to help!"

"Help? Help yourself? What kind of help can you give anybody? I don't have the time to deal with you, Werth. Keep out of it, I warn you!"

Hearns stomped out of the house.

Willy and Nan looked at the door. After a moment they heard a car scream away.

Nan said, "Well, that's that."

Oblivious to her, Willy walked to the nearest window to try to look after the departing car. "He's really something. Can you imagine a man coming into this house and behaving like that? Someone who is supposed to be a responsible person. I don't like to say it but it's just the kind of thing you're led to expect from a cop. Damn cops."

Nan frowned.

"He's got no legal ground to stand on, you realize that, I hope," Willy said. "I may not know about some things, but I know the statutes about private detectives."

"Willy..."

"And as long as I'm not taking money, I can ask people what I like. As long as I don't pretend to be a policeman or use force or deception. Citizens are allowed to ask other citizens questions. It's called free speech. There's no way he can stop me doing that." Symbolically Willy waved a fist after Hearns.

"You are going to give it up, though, aren't you?"

"Goddamn cop! Willy called. "Makes me mad." He turned to her. "Did you say something?"

"You are going to give it up, aren't you? You're not going to go on with this Larry Brinker business. You aren't, are you, Willy?"

"I sure am!"

"Not really—?"

"You just try to stop me."

"Don't be stupid."

"What do you mean?" He fixed her, challenged her as if he'd had another opportunity with Hearns.

She saw he had no intention of relenting. Quietly she said, "There's nothing in it for you but trouble."

"It's a matter of principle now."

"That's ridiculous."

"No megalomaniac detective sergeant is going to interfere with my constitutional rights."

"You're absurd when you get like this."

"Well, then you keep out of it, too."

"How am I supposed to keep out of it when your principles bring angry policemen into my home? Haven't you got sense enough to be able to tell anymore when something is wrong?

You live in a real world. You're not Hank."

"I never said I was. But my business is my business. That's all there is to it."

"Is that all you have to say about it?"

"Yes. Except that I'm going out!"

Imitating Hearns, Willy marched out of the house. He went to his car in the garage, and with a slight slipping of tires as he accelerated down the drive, he drove off.

Willy drove until he came to a shopping center where, impulsively, he turned into the parking lot and parked. He walked to a drugstore and bought a newspaper. At the checkout he asked where the nearest place to get a cup of coffee was.

"There's a machine in the J Mart."

It was nearly half a mile. Willy fumed all the way, but when he got there he found some chairs and tables and a cluster of food machines. Not including a fruit vendor.

He sat with an unwholesome collection of coffee, soup and cookies. The physical relief of taking the load off his feet was unexpectedly great.

He thumbed through the paper, noticed nothing on Larry Brinker and then found the motor-services display ads. He had a look through to see what was available today in secondhand mobile homes.

He found it in the advertisement for Phun Trailers, Your Vacation Specialist on Pendleton Pike. "A '73 Tow-EZ, a sight for sore eyes at $748.98."

Willy studied the ad carefully. Then left without finishing his soup.

Phun Trailers was an altogether less prosperous-looking place than Brinker's Mobile Homes. And the compact vacation trailers looked altogether more mobile than the mobile homes.

As he stepped from his car, Willy was approached by a brightly dressed young man, bald with a beard, who said, "Hello, sir, hello! What can I show you today?"

"My interest," Willy said, "is in the Tow-EZ you advertised today."

"Ahhh," the man said. "I can see you have a shrewd eye for a bargain."

"I don't want to buy it," Willy said. "I want to see it."

"Shop first, decide later. You have a knowledge of the ways of the world, sir, I can tell that."

"I'm not a customer or a potential customer."

The man's manner became immediately more formal. "Who are you then? Advertising standards or what?"

"I am investigating a murder," Willy said.

"Are you a cop?"

"I'm not a cop."

The man scratched the side of his head above his ear. Then pulled on selected hairs in his beard. He decided not to press for classifications, but said, "Well, my time is valuable."

"So is mine," Willy said.

"What about the Tow-EZ then? It's not hot, if that's what you want to know. We don't touch hot stuff, never have."

"I'm following up a lead. I am looking for a Tow-EZ that the owner was trying to sell in a hurry a few days ago. It was six or seven years old and it had paintings and decorations on the outside."

"Well, the description sounds all right."

"Can I see it?"

The salesman took Willy to see it.

The Tow-EZ was a festive sight indeed. It was aerosoled in a dozen different colors, abstractly but pleasantly.

"Well, well," Willy said. He was sure that he had found the trailer that Larry Brinker had argued over the day he was killed.

"The contemporary touch," the salesman said lightly. Then he laughed. "Hell, I'd respray it if it was earlier in the season, but getting it late I thought I'd have a shot at moving it the way it is. It doesn't look too bad to me. Personally, I kind of like it. Not that I'd tow it around, but somebody might. No, they did a good job on it."

"Who did?" Willy asked.

"Whoever did it. Hey, it's about time we talked money, isn't it? You can't expect me to give up good time for nothing." The man scratched the side of his head again.

"The police wouldn't pay you anything."

"You ain't police."

"They'll be interested when I tell them."

"So tell them."

Willy took out his wallet. "Couple of bucks do it?"

"This is now, not a hundred years ago."

"Five, that's my limit."

"What's five bucks these days? I was thinking more like twenty."

"Five bucks is more than no bucks," Willy said stiffly. He held out the fiver.

The man took it.

Suddenly Willy felt uneasy, a little out of his depth. He had a vision of trying to explain to a tax auditor an expense like this entered as a research deduction. Especially without a receipt.

"I want a receipt," Willy said.

The salesman seemed astonished.

"That's the way it's done in real life," Willy assured him. "Nothing is ever as easy as it is in the movies."

Willy provided a piece of paper and the man wrote out a receipt, headed unembarrassedly, "For information supplied."

"All right, now tell me about the guy that sold it to you," Willy said. "Hippie type with long blond hair, am I right?"

"No," the salesman said. "Middle-aged guy with white hair."

"Come on, this is serious. No jokes, if you don't mind."

"I'm not joking. I bought it from a middle-aged guy."

"Oh. When?"

"A few days ago. Last weekend?"

"Do you know who you got it from? Was it a trade-in or something like that?"

"No, straight sale, in the trade."

"In the trade? You mean from another dealer?"

"Yeah."

"Well, who?"

"Guy called Barry Youngman. Works for a place on West Washington called Brinker's."

Willy could hardly contain himself as he drove home.

Nan had her coat on and carried a piece of paper, which she waved at Willy as he came in. "You didn't take my keys, did you?" she asked.

"Sit down while I tell you what's happened," Willy said, taking her by the shoulders. She resisted. "I've made a break-through. I've got to go see Hearns with it. A bit of luck, I guess, but that's the way these things go."

Nan stood, irritated by being held.

"It's about the trailer, did I tell you? Some kid everybody

calls a hippie, he tried to sell it to Larry on—"

"You had a phone call," Nan said. She waved the piece of paper in Willy's face.

"What?"

"I wrote the message. Just after you left. A Miss Barbara Brinker called."

"Boo?"

"So she is known to her intimates, I believe. Miss Brinker asks that you call upon her."

"Go out there?"

"So I would assume."

"Did she say what about?"

"I think," Nan said with pleasure she felt guilty about showing, "that Miss Brinker will request you to give up the foolish preoccupation you have with the death of her father."

"What?"

"I did not put the idea into what she calls her mind, if that is what you are wondering. We did not converse for an extended period."

"What I do is my business," Willy said.

"So you keep telling the world. But I hope you don't expect me to visit you."

Dully, Willy couldn't keep from asking, "Where?"

"In jail. And another thing."

"What?"

"I'm sure you wouldn't have forgotten," heavily, "but your daughter and her husband are coming tomorrow."

"They are? What for?"

"To visit, my dear, to visit. I told you I was going to invite them."

"You did?" Vaguely something clicked.

"I did."

"Well, how long are they staying?"

"Just the day. They'll go back late afternoon. I have a feeling Angel might be pregnant. I told you."

"Oh yeah."

"Something is up, I know that. I can tell from her voice. Do you expect to have any time available from your investigative schedule? Or will you be using what there is to scribble a few words in a letter to your agent to explain why you've given up writing to hang out your shingle as a private detective?"

"Very funny."

"Not funny at all. Dear. But please don't trouble yourself. I will entertain your daughter and her husband—"

"The Crud."

"You remember him! Oh, what a good sign. They say isolated bits of memory coming back herald complete recovery in patients who have forgotten who they are."

"Very funny."

"But don't you bother about us. I shall entertain them, and if you should miss meals I'll try to leave some scraps in a bowl by the door for you. So come and go as you please."

"I'll do what I can," said Willy tamely.

"Oh good!"

Then he couldn't help asking, "Did Boo say when I should come out?"

"I believe she said she was free now," Nan said. "After eight she charges."

As he drove, Willy felt agitated. Part of him thought he ought to call Hearns immediately, but the fact of Hearns's hostility, the vision of Hearns's fury, made him dither.

His thoughts turned to worry about what Boo had called for. Whether it had been a call made on her mother's behalf again. Willy had a sense of things moving too fast, of getting swept up in something he couldn't cope with.

At a crossroads he nearly pulled out directly into the path of an oncoming car.

At a telephone booth in the center of Castleton he stopped. If he had a dime, he would try Hearns.

He had a dime.

Hearns wasn't there.

"Can I have his home phone number?"

"Only he can give that out. Look, why don't you give me your name; I'll try to get him to call you back."

"I'm not at home," Willy said, feeling distinctly seedy.

"Well, let me put you through to Detective Sergeant Malalicky. He's covering tonight."

"No, no, forget it."

"Hang on a minute."

Willy hung up.

With relief, Willy recognized Boo as the Brinkers' door was opened.

"Oh. Mr. Werth!"

"My . . . Nan, she said you wanted me to come out."

"She didn't know when you'd be back, so I didn't expect it was going to be tonight after all."

"Is it all right?" Willy asked. He felt a degree of weariness about the question. The drive to Castleton suddenly felt boring, the mission not compelling.

"Oh yeah. Sure," she said. "Come on in."

"The message wasn't detailed," Willy said. "Is there some problem?"

"Go on into the living room, will you? I just want to check where Mom is."

Boo was gone for what seemed like several minutes. It reminded Willy of waiting for Hearns at headquarters.

Willy sat quietly. He felt no curiosity about the fine possessions that peppered the room. His mind wandered, staying longest on an episode with The Crud. Angela had just brought him home for a weekend and "the men" had been out fishing together. It was something Willy hadn't done for some years and he'd at first been pleased with his remembered competence and The Crud's own easygoing attitude. Then a snapping turtle had taken Willy's line. He'd reeled it in and set about to kill it, cut its head off with a dull knife the way his uncle had taught him in morning lake mists in the misty past. But The Crud had stepped in, cleared the hook and hurled the beast by the shell, so that it skipped along the surface of the fresh lake like a flat pebble. He'd tried to make Willy feel guilty. Willy never forgave him.

Boo was standing before him. "I just wanted to check that Mom was out of the way."

"What? Oh." Willy stood up quickly, as if woken. Boo stepped back in surprise.

"Is something wrong, Mr. Werth?"

"I . . . no. I don't know," Willy said. He had gathered himself. "You tell me."

They both sat.

"I've been thinking," Boo began, somewhat unconvincingly. "I don't think it's such a good idea for you to investigate my father's death after all."

Though he'd been warned, it shocked Willy to hear Boo say it. "Why not?"

Boo hesitated.

Willy said, "Your mother certainly seemed eager for me

to help when I talked to her."

"Yeah. I know."

"Has she changed her mind?"

"No."

"Well, come on, my dear!"

Boo laughed.

Willy watched for a moment. "What's funny?"

"I don't think I've been called 'my dear' for a hundred years."

Willy felt a wave of irritation. "Cut the crap, Boo. You have something you want to say and I am entitled to know what it is."

Boo stopped laughing and sat up straight. Willy's sharpness concentrated her mind wonderfully. "Look, Mr. Werth, I just thought that maybe if you did investigate and turned something up, it might be something that might hurt my mom, see? I mean Dad is dead and after the funeral tomorrow maybe it's best that she just tries to forget about it all, you know?"

"You don't want to find out what happened? Catch who did it?"

"It won't bring him back. So if it might hurt more, what's the point?"

Willy leaned back and studied her. "Why don't you tell me what's happened?"

"Nothing. I just thought about it. That's all. Honest."

"I don't believe you."

Boo thought about this reaction. Broke into a smile. "O.K., maybe a little something."

"What?"

"I think my father had a friend."

"A friend?"

"You know. An outside romantic interest."

"Did you find a letter or something like that?"

She thought about saying no. "Yes."

"Ah."

"Dad had a kind of study here in the house where he did work, but he would listen to music and things. Well, I was going through his cassettes in his desk drawer, and there was this one that wasn't labeled."

"A tape?"

"No, no, don't get yourself excited," she said formally. "It was the cassette container thing. I opened it up and there were these notes."

"I see."

"Well," Boo said. "You see what I mean."

"Not necessarily."

"Oh, come on! They may have been typed on Country Lake stationery but they weren't about any business. They were all about missing him, and why did he have to take vacations, and full of nicknames. It was strictly bed-talk stuff."

"Who were they from?"

"It didn't say. They weren't signed. But they wouldn't have to be, would they?"

"What is Country Lake?"

"A trailer park Dad had a part in."

"You better let me have the letters, Boo."

"I burned them," she said.

Willy didn't believe her. "Either me or the police."

"Look, Mr. Werth, I didn't tell you to give them to you or anybody. No way. You can see, can't you, that my mom wouldn't want to know about things like that?"

Lorraine Brinker breezed into the room. "About things like what?" she demanded cheerfully and undeniably. "What sort of things wouldn't I want to know about?"

"I was telling Mr. Werth here about how I was stopped for speeding yesterday and nearly got a ticket. But the cop was so sweet, and he let me off with a warning. Only he pinched my bottom. I was saying that wasn't the kind of thing you really wanted to hear about."

"You always drive too fast," Lorraine Brinker said. "But, Boo, why didn't you tell me Willy was here?" She walked to him and took his hands. He rose to meet her. "Willy, so kind of you to come out tonight before the funeral, but don't worry. I'll be all right. I'm quite prepared. But I do wish you'd change your mind and come."

"I'm afraid it's impossible," Willy said, picking up his cue nearly as fluently as Boo. He didn't remember what had been said about the funeral.

"Arthur is going to make the most wonderful speech about Larry. I'm sure he will. I know you would have wanted to make one yourself, and probably every bit as good as the one Arthur will make, but he is family, you know. You understand."

"Of course."

"No hard feelings?"

"Of course not."

"You won't hold it against poor little Lorraine?"

"I don't know why you think I would."

"And how is the case going?" she asked, as if her question followed his answer in a direct line of thought.

Willy hesitated.

Boo said, "It's going pretty slow, Mom, he was just saying."

"I thought you were saying about speeding, dear."

"I mean before that. You don't think I'd talk about speeding before I asked him how the case was going, do you?"

"Is that so, Willy? Is it going slowly?"

"Slowly," Willy said, "I'm afraid it is." It could always speed up later. "Though today I've come up with a couple of leads which may be worth following."

Boo frowned severly.

Loraine said, "That's good. But I don't want you to worry about it going slowly. I trust you. You'll get it right in the end. And now I'm afraid that I've got to tear myself away, Willy dear. I've got to get ready to go out and I expect Boo will as well. You don't mind if I ask you to leave, do you?"

"Not at all. Not at all."

Lorraine Brinker pulled him by the hands toward the door. Willy left.

Willy drove nominally in the direction of home.

But his mind churned faster than the car's engine, and took him farther.

In a stroke, less than day, he had become inundated with new information. He didn't know what to do. He felt he ought to know what to do but he didn't. He didn't even know whether he was still on the case or not. Or if he wasn't, whether he should stay on it anyway.

He pulled in at a bar intending to get a drink.

There was a telephone booth outside.

He stood and looked at it for a minute. Decided that if it worked he would make a call. He picked up the receiver, heard an electrical connection that promised a dial tone and he went into the bar for change.

"I'll be back in a minute," he told the barman.

The call he had in mind was to Boo, to tell her about the breakthrough with the Tow-EZ. It was relevant, important. It would show her that the case might well not come to involve her father's friend.

If anything, the Tow-EZ evidence pointed suspicion at Barry Youngman, presumably. Buying and selling behind her father's back. It certainly explained why Youngman had been at great pains to minimize interest in the hippie kid. And it explained a remark of Shifty Shilton's. "A trailer on the side . . . I'm the straight one."

Youngman might have been deflecting attention only because of the extracurricular business. But if Larry hadn't known about such dealings, had only found out that day . . .

Well it was worth telling Boo.

But when Willy called, the phone wasn't answered. He hadn't expected that at all. He hung up, then remembered Lorraine had said she would be going out.

It left Willy feeling totally isolated. Phones ought to get you through when it was important. But they hadn't. Either to Boo or Hearns.

Willy felt confusion, tension. Contradiction.

While he was in the booth, he looked in the telephone directory and found number and address for Barry Youngman. And then for Country Lake Estates.

Youngman could be at home by now. He didn't know whether to go there or not.

Country Lake Estates was over the county line in Hendricks County. It seemed a long way away.

Willy thought about calling Nan.

Instead he pushed out of the phone booth toward the door of the bar.

And stopped.

He remembered the letters. Boo said she'd burned them. He knew she hadn't. But he wondered whether now she might.

She had clearly been displeased when he told her mother he had found a couple of leads. If she took that badly, she might very well go and burn the letters.

And whether she gave the letters to him or to Hearns, they were evidence and shouldn't be destroyed.

Willy was suddenly aware that only he knew about them and the risk of their destruction.

But the Brinkers had just now not answered the phone. Boo would hardly have had time to burn the letters since Willy left. She was going out, too, had gone, since she wasn't the type to let the phone ring and not pick it up.

But when she got back?

The urgency of the situation overwhelmed Willy.

• • •

He drove too fast to Castleton. He didn't know how long they would be out.

It was only as he approached the house that he began to wonder about technicalities. Where he should park. How he would get in.

He drove up the hill past the house. At an intersection a quarter of a mile beyond it, he pulled to the side and thought.

The risk of it all was terrible to him. The idea of a neighbor calling the police, having seen him prowling around . . . the idea of trying to explain to the police what he was doing . . . the idea of being taken down to headquarters, since he wouldn't want to say anything until he'd talked to Boo . . .

Yet . . .

The only way to go, he decided, was to park in front of the house and behave for all the world as if he had every right to be there. Try the front door, walk around the house and see if he could find a window unlatched in a place shielded from view.

He turned the car around. His hands began to shake.

The idea of getting caught, of having to explain it all to Nan . . .

As he approached the house, he felt an urge to drive by. But he hit the curb in front of the house and parked.

And if nothing was unlocked, what then? He could try a credit card on the door locks. He tried to remember what kind of lock there was on the front door. He tried to remember whether he knew anything about the back door.

He took two credit cards out of his wallet. Should he be carrying identification? There was no real alternative. And if arrested, should he say nothing or try to talk his way out of it?

Or should he go away altogether and plan it better?

He got out of the car. Lorraine or Boo might come home at any time. He didn't know what they had gone out for at all.

He took a step toward the house and found his legs shaking underneath him. What he was proposing to do was illegal and dangerous.

The sort of thing he might write about but just not the sort of thing Willy Werth ever did.

Willy got back in his car and drove away.

"Willy. Willy!"

He stirred on the bed.

"Willy! Wake up! It's quarter to eleven."

"Yeah?" Christ.

"They just called, Willy. They'll be here in a couple of minutes. You ought to get up."

"Who will be here?"

"Brock and Angela! Oh God, don't you listen to anything?"

"Oh yeah." Willy rolled his feet off the bed and sat up. "My head hurts," he said.

"I'm not surprised," Nan said stiffly. "They called from a drugstore on Thirty-eighth Street. They'll only be a few minutes."

Willy found some clothes.

As he dressed, Nan said, "And she isn't pregnant."

"Huh?"

"Angela isn't pregnant. I thought she might be, but she isn't."

"How do you know that?"

"Because they have a new car. She told me; she couldn't wait, even though Brock wants to surprise us."

"Hang on," Willy said, hanging on to his trousers.

"That's what I heard in her voice. Come on, Willy, don't just stand there."

"No need to shout," he mumbled.

He followed her down the stairs.

A few minutes later, a red Triumph sports car swerved into the driveway and screamed to a stop. Angela jumped out and ran toward her mother, who was coming to meet her. They hugged. Through the kitchen window Willy watched The Crud unroll his six-foot-six frame from the cockpit. Against all inclination, Willy went out to meet the visitors.

"Hello, Daddy!" Angela said from her mother's shoulder.

"Hello, Angel."

"We got here in only two hours and fifty minutes, even with the stop, and not a cop to be seen!" boomed The Crud. "Hey, big Willy! How you doing, buddy? How you doing?" He pushed past the womenfolk, took Willy's unoffered hand and slapped Willy's back with a meaty paw. "How d'ja like to go for a spin in the new flying machine, huh?"

"I'd love to," Willy said. "But I've got some work I have to do."

Inside the house Nan made coffee and Willy took his without milk.

"How is your book going, Daddy?" Angela asked. "Mother says it isn't going very well."

"It's going fine, just fine," Willy said.

"You just hang in there and keep plugging," The Crud said heartily. He punched Willy supportively on the shoulder.

"Cut it out!" Willy said sharply. The Crud's forms of familial contact left him feeling the victim of an assault.

"Touchy, huh?" The Crud offered jovially. "One too many last night, huh?" The Crud laughed.

"Try to contain yourself, Brock," Angela said hopefully. "Just because you're in a good mood doesn't mean everybody else in the world is."

"I know he's moody, hon, but I try to spread a little light wherever I go," he said. But he wrapped his self-satisfied grin around a coffee cup. ·

"He says his book is going fine," Angela said to Nan.

"Your father knows best about his own work," Nan said.

"Speaking of work," Willy said, "I've got to do some either now or later. And as I didn't expect you two so early, it will probably disrupt plans less if I go up now, don't you think?"

"Hey, big Willy, can you really just turn on the old muse like that?"

"Oh yes," Willy said. He felt utterly empty and was inspired to do nothing but escape. Nan knew this, and he knew she knew.

"You look a bit rough, all the same," The Crud continued. "Why don't you let me get your blood circulating first? How about a little ride?" He jangled keys.

"No thanks."

Nan, sympathetic in the presence of their child, came to Willy's aid. "Yes, Willy, you go on up now. We'll see you a bit later."

"I'll keep the engine warm, big Willy," The Crud said. "We hit a hundred and thirteen on the way here."

"Hit a hundred and thirteen what?" Willy asked.

20

How long have I been sitting here?

Jesus, thirty-five minutes.

Daydreaming. At least I ought to hit the automatic space bar to make it sound like I am typing.

But Nan would know. The sound would be too regular.

Not that I mind, but...

I mind.

If I ought to do anything, I ought to try to write something.

Dear Clarence,

Just a note to warn you that I might—might—be late with the current manuscript. Or if I am on time, it will be too short and that will be the same as being late. Or if it's not too short, it won't be very good. So what's the point?

Yes, I do remember how important the deadline is so that we hit the best spring and book-club slots. Yes, my memory is not impaired, despite what Nan says about my condition last night.

Yes, I had one too many. Or two, but I got change for the phone at the bar in this place and felt obligated to reward the barman for not giving me a hard time about it. And I ran into these guys and got talking about prewar Indianapolis. It stimulated my memory, gave me a lot of stuff and was useful.

No, I can't remember anything just at the moment but...

Yes, I can. There was this time when I was a kid

and I came to the table dressed up in my wild-West
suit: Stetson and chaps and guns; Ma played along
and dished my food out from "the chuck wagon." But
Charlie took one look at me and said, "You're not
really a cowboy."

That really shot me down. Boy, it really did.

My introduction to self-perception and reality and
stuff.

Charlie is my brother. He's the linear thinker in
the family. I'm the lateral one.

It brought back other stuff, too. Christ, the prewar
time was lively. People were carrying on about the
Stutz Car Company closing. And Paul V. McNutt. But
even at that tender age (sixteen) I was finding out
about beer as a chaser. And what it chased.

It did some chasing last night, old son. I can tell
you.

But HANK lives. It's just his creator is finding it
harder to kill people than he used to.

Why did I write that last bit. I never thought that
before.

I don't think I could bear writing this letter. Maybe
I ought to Hank it out. Where was I? God, my head.
Oh, yeah. He was in The Doodah making love. I mean
making plans.

"Like what happened to Stella McKeand," I said.
"We're off to see about that."

"But what can we do here?" Mossman asked me
with her doe eyes shimmering like limpet pools.

Uh.

"We can..."

Uh.

"We can go see the key to this whole business.
Woodrow McKeand."

"What is he like?"

"He's the kind of little guy that collects art and

smokes a cigar and sends a bozo to my office with instructions to bring me back to see him. At first I thought he was a businessman who played at looking like a gangster, but I got it the wrong way round."

"Don't," she said.

"Don't what?"

"Don't get any ideas about dropping me off and leaving me out of it."

She was reading my mind. Not bad. Halfway to a good woman.

"You don't think I brought you all the way over here to pack you away someplace," I said.

"Just don't," she said. "I'm in."

*　　*　　*

I knew better than to look for McKeand at home. It was nighttime, so he'd be in his office behind the kitchen of his restaurant.

"Hungry?" I asked.

She squinted at me. "Sure," she said.

I had to laugh.

I drove to McKeand's restaurant.

His ugly red Triumph was in the parking lot.

CHAPTER XXIV

"Take me to see McKeand."

"Watcha think you doing, busting in here? You oughtn't ta do that. You gotta wait out in the restaurant like everybody is supposed to."

The pug filled the doorway in front of me. He was wide enough to fill French windows, but there weren't any handy. But I was tired of supposed-tos, oughtas, and gottas.

"Out of the way, you crud. My head hurts with everything that's been happening, and if you don't move now I'll damn well stack you in the corner and put a 'This side up' sign on you 'cause nobody will be able to tell otherwise."

"Haw. You and who else?"

"Me and the lady here," I said, giving a slight and effete bow in Mossman's direction.

"Haw. Haw. Haw," he said.

He wasn't laughing.

I buried my right fist in the flab of his belly. My left is good but my right is better.

The pug's head came down to me like an executioner's axe. But it wasn't an attack. He was stacking himself for me. All I needed was the "This side up" sign.

I gave the head a two-hand chop as it went past. It was a bit excessive, but I was feeling mean. I'm moody that way.

The pug's head poured down toward the ground and found the floor where the gap between his fleshy legs was. He did a somersault and nearly prosecuted Mossman with his heels as he completed his turn.

He was unconscious and gasping for breath.

"Men, women—I leave 'em all like that," I said. "The technique may be different but the result is the same."

She was full of admiration. I could tell.

I walked through and pushed open McKeand's door.

Woodrow McKeand sat at his desk puffing on a huge black cigar. He held a sawed-off shotgun. It was pointed at my belly.

"The way I feel," I said, "the pellets would just bounce off, and come back at you with twice the speed. So be careful who you try to waste with that thing."

"Midwinter!" He looked surprised to see me.

"Surprised to see me?"

"I . . . Of . . . of course." He raised his hands to wipe the sweat off his brow. Only it didn't work because he forgot to put the shotgun down first. "You're supposed to be in England," he said, finding words. "With my wife."

Mossman walked in behind me.

"That's not my wife," he said. He looked pale.

"Right first time," I said. "It's not your wife. Your wife has been murdered."

"Murdered," he repeated, but without questioning it.

"Murdered. Terminated. Made dead. And I am here to solve who did it."

The shotgun dropped from his hand. The stock hit an arm of his chair. The gun went off.

21

As Willy began to think of stopping, he heard a car pull out of the driveway. It decided him. He came downstairs hungry, but pleased with himself. It had been one of those sessions when he'd been so certain the work would go badly that he'd relaxed and it had gone well. And as a reward he had the house to himself. Great.

He walked into the kitchen and was at the refrigerator door before he realized, with a shock, that he was not alone.

"Hey, hey, big Willy," The Crud said enthusiastically. "How you doing?"

"I thought you'd gone," Willy said. He didn't turn to face his son-in-law.

"Nope. The girls went off and left me to take care of you. You looked so bad I didn't think you ought to be left alone."

Willy opened the refrigerator.

"What you got in there? I could eat a little something, too."

Willy took out a bottle of soda water and a piece of processed cheese. The Crud walked over, but watched Willy sit at the breakfast table before he inventoried the refrigerator for himself. "Feeling the effects, eh, big Willy?"

"Yes," Willy said. He drank from his soda water.

"My dad always said—"

"I don't want to know what your dad always said or even what he sometimes said."

"He had a sure cure for hangover."

"Teetotalism. I don't want to know."

The Crud waggled his head affably. "You got a lot on your mind. I can understand."

"What do you know about my mind?"

"You're poking around in this murder of this friend, right?"

"Who told you about that?"

"Well, Angy, she got it off her mom and I got it off Angy. Among other things." He laughed merrily and took out some tomatoes, ham, mustard, fruit and bread. "I hate that processed stuff, I don't know how you can eat it," he said. "So how you doing on the case? Found out who done it yet?"

Willy said nothing. He nibbled his cheese.

It came back to him that he had been taken off the case.
Or nearly. Or something. And that he had found the trailer.
And that Boo had letters from her father's friend. Unless she'd
destroyed them.

It had all left his mind.

"No, look, big Willy," The Crud continued. "I admire you
for it. It's gotta take nerve to get in there and mix it with cops
and relatives and that. Fine, it may be stuff you'll write a book
about sometime, but if you're out looking for a murderer there's
got to be a chance that you're going to find him. And that
means you could get into a fix yourself. Hell, I'm not telling
you anything you don't know already, but that takes a kind of
nerve. I admire you for it, I really do."

Risk of physical danger had never crossed Willy's mind.
"I'm glad," he said.

"Especially since it's costing you so much money." The
Crud sat down heavily on a chair across the table.

"Money?"

"Nan told Angy this morning how much time you're giving
up."

"I'm not giving up anything," Willy said testily.

"No? Nan said you were. Huh. Funny." He ate.

"What does she know?"

"I don't know," The Crud said in the middle of a bite. "I
was just trying to admire you."

"Thanks for nothing."

"O.K., O.K. If you don't want to talk, you only got to say
so, sport. It's your maison. You seen the morning paper?"

"No," Willy said. "I haven't had a morning yet." He picked
up his soda water and carried it through to the living room.
He sat facing the picture window and looked at the trees blow-
ing in the gentle wind outside. His head began to hurt. He
spilled some soda water in his lap and felt irritated. He couldn't
remember exactly how his situation with the Brinkers had been
left.

Which meant, he decided, that it hadn't been left exactly.

Screw it. He still had the authorization from Boo. Hank it
out.

Some early birds flew south in a flock.

It came back to Willy that he had already been told about
one friend of Larry's. A. Smith, the delicate tennis partner.

Willy sat up. Boo had said a friend, but the gender wasn't

specified. He didn't know whether she knew or whether it hadn't crossed her mind that it might be in question.

It hadn't crossed Willy's mind, until now.

Resolutely he left the living room and walked up the stairs to his office phone.

The Crud said something as he went up, but Willy didn't hear what.

On the stairs Willy remembered the antiques in the Brinker household. A friend in antiques?

He dialed the number.

There was no answer. He hung on. He thought for a moment.

The funeral.

He hung up.

He realized he ought to go to the funeral.

But he didn't want to.

He sat at the desk feeling trapped. His head hurt.

Without thinking any more about it, he picked up the sheets he had been working on less than an hour before.

22

The gun went off, both barrels. The explosion seemed to fill the room in my head. I caught pellets in my cheek, ricochets, one just below the right eye. I jumped at the guy and pulled the weapon away. I shouted at him. I lifted the gun up to crack him one back, just below his eye.

Mossman pulled at the shotgun in my hands.

I held on, glaring at McKeand. He cowered in his chair.

I had nearly scared him to death, which would have been a first.

But I let Mossman take the gun. McKeand had talking to do. I'd settle whether he lived or died after.

"Are you all right?" Mossman asked.

"Yeah."

She dabbed at my cheek with a handkerchief. She was very gentle. The handkerchief smelled of roses.

"You look it," she said.

I assessed myself. Clothes torn in several places, from small clusters of shot. Bleeding from face, an arm and two legs. "All in the line of work," I said. "How about you?"

"I'm fine."

I looked her over. She looked pretty good. Our eyes met, and held. I knew then she was something special in my life.

McKeand moaned.

"You could have told him a little more delicately," Mossman said to me at last.

"Or I could have written him a letter." I turned back to McKeand. "But the crazy little bastard isn't upset because his wife is dead."

I had McKeand's attention again.

And Mossman's.

"Are you, Woodrow?" I picked him up by the armpits. "Are you?"

His eyes squinted, then bugged out with a crazy glaze. But he didn't say anything.

"See, he wasn't surprised that I was back from England now," I continued. "He was surprised that I could come back at all."

Mossman was puzzled.

I was angry.

I shook McKeand. "You didn't plan for me to come back, did you?"

"You shouldn't be here," he managed to say.

"You expected me to be getting strung up by the English cops for your wife's murder."

McKeand was silent.

Mossman was thunderstruck. "You mean he knew about it?"

"I mean he ordered it," I said.

23

Willy came down the stairs quietly. He bent forward at the bottom to listen for signs of life. He heard none, straightened and walked into the kitchen.

"It's your father playing cowboys-and-Indians," Nan said lightly behind him.

Willy turned to see Nan and Angela following him down the hall from the living room.

"It's Wrong Way Willy, the half-gun slinger from wild-West Indy."

"Are you enjoying yourself?" Willy asked.

"Hi, Daddy," Angela said. "You've been working a long time."

"Yes," Willy said. "I have."

"I'm sure," Nan said.

Willy ignored it. "Did you do good shopping? Or whatever it was you went out for."

"I'm surprised, if you've been working so hard, that you noticed we were out."

"Zip it up, will you?"

"If you'll stop posturing about working yourself to a frazzle. We found your glass in the living room. Have you done anything at all?"

"I'll see you later," Willy said. "Unless my luck holds." He marched toward the back door, but paused to say to Angela, "I'm sorry your mother is in the kind of mood she is, dear. We'll have a bit of a visit later on, O.K.?"

He left.

Near the garage Willy found The Crud, who was bouncing around the driveway pretending to dribble and shoot a basketball.

"Hey, hey, hey, big Willy!"

"You sound like Yogi Bear."

"Who?"

"Oh, forget it."

"You ought to put up a basket out here, you know that? It

would give you something to do to work off your hostilities when you were feeling kind of, you know—"

"Hostile?"

"That's it."

"I never feel hostile. Only violent."

"Oh," said The Crud. "Oh. Well." He dropped a short jumper. "You know, I was hurt this morning."

"Oh?"

"When you were so bad-tempered. But I just wanted to say that I understand. Artistical temperament and all that." He faked right and drove left.

"I have the same temperament as an accountant," Willy said.

"You do?"

"Yes. Definitely."

"It's just," The Crud said, "that I'm so sensitive to bad feeling. It kind of wants to make me go out and kick leaves, only there aren't enough leaves around in August. So I decided to come out and shoot baskets, only there isn't one. You know the kind of feeling I mean?"

Willy knew exactly what The Crud meant and would never have believed him capable of meaning anything of the kind. Willy began to feel rotten about being swinish to The Crud.

"I'm sorry about earlier on, Brock," Willy said haltingly.

"Oh hell," The Crud said heartily. "Don't think nothing of it." He clapped Willy hard on the shoulder. "Hey, hey, big Willy."

"Well, I've got to—"

"Hey, there was something else I wanted to say."

"Yeah?" Willy asked.

"I wanted to say I could give you some help."

"Help? You?"

"It's just if you are in some kind of money trouble, what with work being so hard and everything, I could probably help out. You know, short-term loan sort of stuff. It's not that I'm rich, but I've had a little luck, getting promoted and all that, so I could probably help you out for a while if you needed it. And we could keep it on the quiet, if you wanted." The Crud winked at him.

"The day I need your help . . ." Willy struggled to find words.

"Any day," The Crud said, "any day at all. A father of Angela's is a father of mine." The Crud chuckled. "Hey, I gotta go in now, but don't forget."

He left Willy quivering, alone on the court.

From a phone booth Willy dialed the Brinkers' number again. His hand was unsteady and he found himself somewhat breathless. He was not really in control and it was uncomfortable. He prepared various things to say to Boo.

Lorraine Brinker answered, "This is Lorraine Brinker."

"Uh," Willy said. "This is Willy—Willy Werth."

"Hello. What can I do for you?" Formal, efficient.

"I just . . . well, it's hard to say."

"Please try."

"It's just I had part of a conversation with Boo yesterday and she seemed to be uncertain whether I should keep working on finding out what happened to Larry, and—"

"Oh, God, Larry!" Lorraine said. "I forgot about him for a moment." She cried for a moment. "The funeral hardly cold and I answer the phone and he goes completely out of my head. I must be the worst wife there ever was, the very worst." She bawled.

"I'm sorry, I'm sorry," Willy said. Nothing else came out. She didn't acknowledge him. He wanted to hang up, to leave her alone, to stop intruding on her grief, but felt he couldn't. Finally there was a lull in her sobbing. "Should I call back another time, Lorraine?"

She cried again.

It seemed like an hour. Willy's head hurt.

Then, suddenly, "What was it about finding things out, William?"

Equally suddenly, Willy felt absurd asking what he called to ask. "It was to make sure that you want me to go on trying to clear up what happened."

"Don't you want to anymore?"

"It's not that," Willy said, slowly. It was Boo he wanted to talk to.

"What is it that Boo said to you?"

"Well, maybe I was reading too much between the lines," protecting Boo now, "but she seemed to suggest that you might have had second thoughts about it."

"Barbara and I have not discussed the subject at all," Lorraine Brinker said.

"I wanted to be reassured," Willy said truthfully, "reassured that I wasn't—wouldn't be intruding if I kept on."

"You keep on, if you want to. By all means."

"Well, it's not exactly if I 'want' to. I mean it's never been like that exactly."

"You don't want to?"

"I was always willing to, if it would be a help."

"And you're not willing to now?"

"Yes, of course I am."

"I don't see the problem. You keep on, if you want to, Willy. You have my permission."

Willy's stomach began to hurt, keeping his head company.

Lorraine picked up the slack. "Why would Boo think I wouldn't want you to find out what happened to Larry? I mean—well, we all know what happened to Larry, but not who did it to Larry."

"Her concern must have been for your feelings," Willy said. "That if things became—turned out not to be quite right, or not what you'd expect, that maybe it would be just as well not to pursue the matter."

Sharply, "What could be less 'quite right' than a murder?"

"I don't know," Willy said. "I don't know nearly enough to know. But the decision for me to help was made pretty quickly. And I thought you ought to have the chance to take me off easily after you'd had a couple of days to think about it, and if maybe you had second thoughts."

"Why should I have second thoughts?"

"My working on the case isn't going to bring him back, and it's possible you'd prefer just to let the past become the past."

"The police are still working on the case, aren't they?"

"Yes."

"So what difference is it if you do, too, if you want to?"

"I don't know," Willy said. "I don't know."

"There's no need to shout at me," Lorraine Brinker said. "I know it won't bring him back." She began to cry again. But stopped. "You keep working on it, if you want to, Willy. You keep working on it for a year, if you want to."

Willy drove out to Country Lake Estates. It was the only place he felt he could go besides home.

Without real cause, he expected it to be hard to locate. But the turns were clearly marked with all-weather blue-and-white arrows.

A mile off the main highway Willy found a village of trailers. Almost all on permanent footings, they followed the shoreline of a small wooded lake like a necklace. Near the entry road stood a pendant of units three and four deep; elsewhere around the lake they were only a few yards from the water's edge. A narrow loop of road ran round the place, widening only where it met the road connecting to the outside; there Willy found a small unit with blue-and-white awnings marked "Office."

There was a graveled parking space alongside this trailer, and Willy pulled in.

Before he cut his motor, a substantial woman, frocked in yellow polka-dotted cotton, came down the office steps.

"Hello, mister," she said as he got out of his car. "My name is Gladys Murray and I'm the manager here. What can we do for you?" Her voice contained the quality of jovial scrutiny more often associated with night watchmen and small-town sheriffs.

The question caught Willy unprepared. Although he should have planned, he wasn't sure what he wanted, or how he should go about things.

He said, "I am trying to locate someone. A tall young man who plays tennis. I think his name is Smith."

Gladys Murray turned hard. "What are you?" she asked eyeing him. "You're not repossession."

"No," Willy said. But faced with a choice of what he was, he opted for what he could defend easily. "I'm a writer and I'm doing research for a book which I think Mr. Smith can help me with."

"There is no Mr. Smith here," she said.

"I think his first initial is 'A.'"

"It doesn't matter what his first initial is, mister," she said. With a practiced smile she spread her hands, making of herself, if not a mountain of a woman, then a hill. "We haven't got any Smiths, it's as simple as that."

Willy didn't know whether to take no for an answer.

"Sorry," Gladys Murray said. She turned to go back to the office.

"Excuse me," Willy said.

The woman stopped and turned back to him slowly.

"Can I ask, did you know Lawrence Brinker?"

Quietly she said, "We all knew Mr. Brinker here. He created Country Lake." She paused and lowered her eyes momentarily.

"He was buried today. Why do you ask?"

"It's just I am trying to help his family find out what happened to him."

Gladys Murray rubbed her mouth. "You're not a writer then?"

"I am, yes," Willy said.

"What's your name?"

"William Werth."

Willy couldn't tell whether she recognized it.

"How are you helping find out what happened to him, Mr. Werth?"

"It's a little insubstantial," Willy said, "but I'm trying to work through things that the police might not have time to follow through."

"What kind of thing?"

Willy flushed, put on the spot. "Background of people involved," he said, pausing to think how to continue.

"Involved?"

"Involved with Mr. Brinker. Like his salesmen and people he . . . knew privately."

She looked dubious. "You're saying the person who killed him was someone who knew him?"

"I'm trying to find out," Willy said.

"And you're writing a book about it?"

"No, no," Willy said. "Not really. I just said that."

Gladys Murray studied him, then shrugged. "Well, there are still no Smiths around here." She turned again and went into the office.

Willy got back in his car. He sat.

His emotions were in a turmoil.

He considered driving around the lake road. He started the car. But instead he drove back toward Indianapolis.

If he had thought about it better, he decided, he would have worked it out before he went out there.

The notes were on Country Lake stationery. The place wasn't a hotel. They didn't put stationery in every desk drawer. The notes had to come from someone who worked there.

He should have known before.

Willy slapped himself on the thigh, a punishment.

Not, he thought, that he could see the woman, Gladys Murray, as having been a part of a scenario involving Larry's murder.

Or could he?

For that matter, could he see her as Larry Brinker's girl friend?

Well, who knows?

I know, Willy thought.

Then wondered if he did.

It occurred to him that other people had access to Country Lake stationery.

Or, for that matter, did the writer have to have independent access to it at all?

If Larry Brinker had gone on vacation and wanted letters while he was away, surely less comment would be made if they arrived looking like business. He could perfectly well have given the stationery to his friend. So his friend could still be absolutely anyone.

Or could it?

Willy couldn't decide.

He thought about going back, asking Gladys Murray directly.

But he had trouble thinking of a convincing reason why it was so important to know.

Except, if she wasn't the friend, the real friend might turn out to be more important to the case than she was.

But by that time he was home.

As he walked in the door, Nan smiled and said, "There you are, dear."

"In person."

"I'm afraid you've missed lunch. We had lamb chops." Willy was known to like lamb chops. "I rescued a couple for you. I can reheat them now, if you're hungry. Or would you like something to drink? Coffee?"

"Coffee would be nice," Willy said.

"Angela and Brock are in the living room."

"Are they?"

Nan took a mug from its hook and poured coffee from the pot.

"Angel's told me," she said.

Willy thought for a moment. "Told you what?"

"About Brock," Nan said warmly. "I think it's very very sweet."

"What could possibly be sweet about Brock?"

"Don't play obtuse, William. It doesn't suit you."

"I'm not playing anything. You say something's sweet about Brock. The Crud couldn't be sweet if he had icing on. I don't know what you're talking about."

"About Brock," Nan said more emphatically, insistent. "About what he said to you this morning."

Willy tried to remember something sweet before noon about The Crud. "I don't . . ."

"About lending us money if we need it," Nan said, exasperated.

"That!" Willy said.

"Yes. He hasn't got so much to spare, so it's a really specially nice gesture and very very sweet."

"But we don't need any money!" Willy was angry now.

"That's not the point."

"It's not?"

"No, it's the offer."

"Oh yes?"

"He's showing us that he's concerned. He's obviously seen how preoccupied you are and he's saying that if it affects—"

"I am not preoccupied and he hasn't got the perception to see it if I was."

"That's ridiculous. I'm increasingly impressed with how sensitive Brock is."

"The only way he understands things is if they're held in front of him in large type and sounded out, syllable by syllable. Which must be just about what you did for him about this business."

"*I* did!"

"It certainly wasn't me."

"Well! I like that!"

"Well, I don't," Willy said.

If he hadn't just come in, he would have stomped out. Instead he stomped up.

24

"He ordered his wife's murder just like he ordered his brother's murder."

"He did?" Mossman asked.

"I suspected he was behind what happened to his brother as soon as he told me about it," I said. "It's a matter of motive. He had the most to gain. But he said it was done by local mobsters and sent me over there, so I went on the off-chance he was telling me the truth. But as soon as I saw the place I could tell that the only kind of mobsters it had was kids who stole hubcaps off bicycles."

"You think you're smart, don't you?" McKeand snarled.

I dropped him onto his chair.

"And then within a few hours after his wife and I got to Frome, she was dead. The only way anybody could know we were going to be there was if he told them. So whatever happened was because he wanted it to happen. It doesn't take somebody from Harvard to work that out."

"You can't prove a thing," McKeand said.

"I won't need to," I said. "All I have to do is spell it out for the cops in words of one syllable and they'll prove it for me."

I looked at him hard.

I was seeing a vivid vision of Stella McKeand, half-headless in the pool of her own coagulating blood. If I could have drowned McKeand in it, I would have. I would have stuffed the clots up his nose.

I was slipping into sentimentality.

It's a trap. It makes you careless. You don't hear things you should.

Like when a man with a gun walks into the room behind you.

CHAPTER XXV

"Well, isn't this a pretty sight."

I pivoted toward the voice, into the borings of a .45 revolver.

"Oh, Hank!" Mossman said. "The voice. That's—"

"Brock Hallett," I told her.

"At your service," Hallett said, with a jagged smile. McKeand grinned death.

I've never been one to stand on ceremony when a gun is pointing in my direction. People who put their hands up are the ones who get bullets in the stomach.

I dived at Hallett across McKeand's desk. It was kind of an elaborate somersault, my hands on the floor and my heels whipping at him.

He shot straight forward. If I'd been right side up, the bullet would have torn my heart away. As it was, the danger went between my legs.

I hit him hard.

He fired again. But the arm was deflected up. The bullet tore a gash in the ceiling. It was a long gash; it was a big bullet.

When I got to him, I led with my right.

The gun went off again, this time very close to my ear.

I knew I didn't have much time.

I heard screams, but saw red. I hit the man again and again and again. I felt like a pneumatic drill, trying to tunnel a hole straight through him, to China.

He resisted for a while.

When he quit, I quit. As he fell back, I didn't have the strength to do anything but fall forward on him.

I could only pant and rest.

Finally I rolled over and got up.

Mossman had the .45. She held it as if she didn't know which end did the damage. It made me wonder if she was a virgin.

It was then I looked at McKeand. He was slumped backward in his chair. Blood oozed from the side of his head.

I looked at Mossman again. She turned toward me.

The gun turned with her.

I had a very uncomfortable time looking up her barrel. If I was wrong about her, if she was in league with Hallet, then I was dead.

She opened her mouth.

Nothing came out.

She tried again. "Here," she said.

I took the gun.

"You...you move quickly."

"Practice makes reflex," I said. "How is McKeand? Is he dead?"

"I...I don't know." But give her credit. She went over to him and looked at the man's head.

"It looks like a cut. Along the side."

"He's breathing?"

"Yes."

Hallett stirred on the floor.

"A graze then."

"I think he ought to have a doctor," Mossman said.

"All right. We'll get the cops to bring one."

"Get me a doctor, too, you filthy son of a bitch." It was Hallett. He had both hands around his middle, hugging himself.

I pointed the gun at him.

"No! No!" he said.

I walked over to him.

He whined.

I kicked him.

The door opened beside me.

The elephantine bodyguard pug barged in. He grabbed the gun in my hand and there was nothing I could do as his other big fat paw smashed into one of my ears.

I didn't actually lose consciousness, but I felt a strong urge to close my eyes and just listen for a while.

"Uh, boss, I'm...Boss! Hey, you, lady, get away from him. What you done to him?"

"I've not—"

"What you done to him! What you done to him!"

To intercede on Mossman's behalf, I decided to tune vision in again. Only it was me the monster pug was

threatening. He had the .45 in his hambone hand. He
made it look like a steel baby bottle about to give me
some milk.

"Ya killed him! Ya killed him!"

"He's not dead," Mossman said somewhere. "He's
alive."

"Ya—" The pug stopped. "He ain't gone yet?"

"He'll be all right," she said. "You come and look."

He squinted at her. "Aw, no. I ain't that stupid.
You're with this guy on the floor. I ain't leavin' him
to get him jumpin' on my back to cause me surprise
again. He caused me surprise one time and it ain't
gonna happen again. You get my boss to talk, lady.
You get him to say he's not dead. I'll believe you
then."

"He's unconscious," Mossman said. "When he wakes
up, he'll talk, but he's breathing. You listen."

We were all very quiet while the monster listened.

"Hell, all I can hear is him." He pointed to Hallett.
"Who the hell is he, anyhow? Who the hell are you?"

"I'll tell you who he is," I said.

For which offer I had my jawbone nearly folded for
packing.

"I asked him to talk hisself," the pug said.

"Keep them from hurting me," Hallett said. He was
simpering but I could tell he was thinking.

"O.K., you," the pug said. "I didn't see you come in. I
want to know what you are doing in this room with
these people that killed my boss."

"He isn't dead," Mossman insisted.

"He is until he ain't," the pug said.

"Look," I said, "there's no need to pursue this
charade if—"

"Shut up! You shut up! I come in here and you had
the gun in your hand and the boss was…like that.
You shut up or I'll shut you up!"

I shut up.

"I don't know who all these people are," Hallett
said. "I arrived in good faith to deliver a message. I
didn't want any trouble and then these people beat me
up and they were going to kill me just like they killed
your boss."

"He isn't—"

"You shut up, lady! I seen dead! I know dead!"

"Please don't hurt me," Hallett whined. "I don't want any trouble."

"I ain't gonna hurt you," the pug said. "I hurt anybody, it's gonna be him."

"Please let me go."

"Don't do that!" I said. "He shot your boss."

"That's crazy," Hallett said. "How could I shoot him when I didn't have the gun?"

The pug absorbed the logic.

"I only came to deliver a message," Hallett said. "That's all, and I just want to go home to my wife and her little baby."

"What message was that?" the pug asked.

"It was that Mr. McKeand's wife was murdered in England and that the police are looking for a man and a woman who did it."

The pug glared at him.

"A man and a woman," Hallett repeated.

The light dawned.

"But please, mister," Hallett sniveled. "Let me go home now, will you? Please!"

"Don't!" Mossman and I shouted together.

But the pug had taken against us for some reason. "Go on," he said. "You go home."

Brock Hallett didn't need freeing twice. He slipped out the door. Mossman and I just looked at each other.

I wondered how the hell I came to be here.

"Now for you two," the pug said.

And then Woodrow McKeand groaned.

The pug's jaw dropped when he realized what the sound was, what it meant. His shooting arm dropped, too, and he went round the desk to his boss's side.

Mossman and I didn't need freeing twice either.

CHAPTER XXVI

I stopped the Doodah at the first phone booth I found. I sent the police to McKeand's. The combination of McKeand's wound and the pug's fingerprints on the

.45 would be enough to keep them on ice until I had
time to drop them into the real hot water.

I went back to the car and turned to my colleague.
"And now for Hallett," I said.

"But he could be anywhere!"

"That," I said, "is our advantage."

"It is?"

"He doesn't know his way around Indianapolis and
he isn't here to do sightseeing. He couldn't afford to
stay in the restaurant if McKeand was dead, but if
McKeand wasn't dead he would have to link up with
him again. The only other place to do that is at
McKeand's house, so that is where Hallett is going to
go. His only problem is that he doesn't know where it
is or how to get there. I figure it will take him
another forty-three minutes. So how would you like to
pass the time?"

She didn't think about it much. "Let's go to
McKeand's early and see what pops up."

25

"For Christ's sake, Willy," Nan said from the doorway, "I've waited for as long as I can, but not only are Brock and Angel leaving, your brother Charlie is here. With his wife."

With his fingers poised over the typewriter keyboard, Willy turned to face her. He thought. Then he took the paper out of the machine and bundled the pages of the day into the desk drawer reserved for current work.

She followed him downstairs.

"Honestly," she said, "some days we can't get you up there at all and some days we can't get you down. You didn't used to be so contrary."

Deb and Charlie were standing in the living room, and as Willy arrived in the hall he turned to them. "How good to see you!" he said, and then was surprised by the warmth he heard in his own voice. "Just let us send off Angela and Brock. Get yourselves a drink, O.K.?"

He pivoted and led Nan to the kitchen.

"Sorry, Dad," Angela said. "But we couldn't wait anymore."

"That's all right, Angel," Willy said.

"Still, it was nice to see Uncle Charlie and Aunt Deborah. Why didn't you tell them to come over earlier?"

"Next time, maybe," Willy said.

"Hey, hey, big Willy!"

Willy turned cautiously to The Crud, but before he could speak Angela said, "Why don't you two come and visit us for a change next time?"

"We wouldn't want to put you out, Angel honey," Willy said.

"But you wouldn't. How about Labor Day? Oh, no, wait a minute, we'll be going to Brock's folks. They always have a big family day on Labor Day."

Still looking at The Crud, Willy said, "Well, maybe Halloween."

Angela didn't reply. In the circumstances a reproof.

"You know better than to take your father seriously," Nan

said. "Bye, now." She turned to The Crud and said, "Thank you for coming over, even if just for a while."

"Besides," Willy said, "If we came to you, it would keep Brock from being able to drive faster than a speeding bullet in his new toy."

The Crud bestowed a lavish goodbye kiss on Nan's cheek and much of the rest of her face. "Thanks a packet for the hospitalidad," he said.

He turned to Willy and took Willy's right hand out of his pocket. He shook it vigorously. "You're a rough diamond," The Crud said. "Bye, Pops."

"I'll Pops you."

"Come on, Ange," The Crud said. "Let's lay some rubber." Blasting the neighborhood with overtures from a klaxon horn, they made their departure.

Nan dabbed at her eyes for a moment, but when they turned back to the house she said, "Why the hell didn't you tell me you'd invited Charlie and Deb?"

"Because I didn't."

Nan accepted this.

At the kitchen door she touched him for a moment on the back of his arm.

Charlie and Deb were on the couch when Nan and Willy entered the living room, but Charlie rose quickly. "I'd like to say, Nan," he said, "that we were just passing through the neighborhood and thought we'd drop in."

"Uh," Nan said.

"I'd like to say that, but it isn't true. We came out specially and not just to escape the termites. Willy and Deb and I had a little mix-up during the week, and I thought it'd be a lot better to meet it face on rather than let it drag out. I spent long enough away from family and without family to have learned that you mustn't let little things get in the way of important things."

Faced so starkly, Willy and Nan were uncomfortable, as if what they had said about Charlie and Deb in private had somehow been discovered writ large in a public place.

"Well, I'm sure," Nan said, "that whatever it was wasn't very—well, you know."

Charlie and Deb stood silent, looking uneasy.

"I'm not being much of a host," Willy said. "Chas, can I get you something to drink?"

Nan said, "Isn't Angela looking well?"

Deb said, "I don't suppose there's anything you want to know about England now, is there, William?"

"What I'd like," Charlie said, slightly after the others, "what I'd really like is for the four of us to go out to dinner. Hey, how about that, Willy? Nan? My little treat, eh?"

Charlie took them to The Sycamores, by repute the most expensive restaurant in Indianapolis. It was certainly one of the most expansive, occupying the full basement of one of the office buildings standing guard around Monument Circle.

The room, as they entered it, was welcomingly cool. It was also welcomingly dark, lit indirectly by optic fiber starbursts that glowed near all the potted sycamores that forested the room.

Charlie had booked a table. It was beneath an inset sub-surface window, which gave the table a view of the illuminated Soldiers and Sailors Monument.

"Quite a structure, I always think," Charlie said to break the silence after they sat. "Impressive."

"It's made of oolitic limestone," Willy said.

"Is it?"

"From Oolitic."

"Pardon?" Deb.

"Oolitic, Indiana. A town, near Bedford."

"Oh."

"They're also supposed to have supplied the stone to face the Empire State Building," Willy said.

"Take my advice," Nan said. "Don't get him started."

"It rather reminds me of Piccadilly Circus," Deb said. "I mean, with the statuary in the middle. There's something reminiscent of it. Did you see Piccadilly Circus while you were over there, William?"

After a pause, Deb said, "Charlie was right when he said you'd been over in England some years ago, wasn't he?"

"I can't say that I remember seeing a circus," Willy said. "But maybe I did. It's been quite a while."

"It's not that kind of circus," Deb said. She seemed about to explain—her body squirming around the effort she made with her mouth—when the wine waiter put them out of a collective misery.

"Now, don't look at the prices," Charlie said. "Do you have menus without prices?"

"Unfortunately, no, sir," the man said.

"Boy, I feel like some champagne," Charlie said. "Anybody else?"

"A stinger," Deb said. "A large one."

A round of various but large cocktails was ordered. The drinks were consumed. The glasses were refilled, re-emptied. The party began to jolly up.

"I've got a little confession to make," Charlie said.

"What's that, ol' bean?" Willy asked.

"We didn't just happen to be passing by when we stopped at your house."

"You already said that, Charlie!" Nan laughed.

"It's our anniversary today," Charlie persisted. "It's our anniversary."

"Charles, don't," Deb said, but she was smiling easily.

"It's the anniversary of the day we met, it is, and I thought, I thought, that's a good . . . anniversary."

"There's something I've always wanted to ask you," Nan said. She leaned across the table to fill Deb's wineglass. "How did you and Charlie really meet? I mean, I know you met outside the country, or something. But you never really said."

"Don' push her abould it," Willy slobbered. "Everyone knows Sharlie was invovved in why slave traffic and she ressued him from it. Maybe she don wan talk boud it."

"Stop talking in that silly voice, Willy," Nan scolded.

Deb burst into unexpected laughter. "What a hoot you are, William. Your books are bizarre but personally you can be a real hoot!"

Nan said, "I better fill my glass, too, so I don't get left out."

"I'll get another bottle," Charlie said.

"Come on. Where did you meet?"

"Tangiers," Willy said.

"Mexico City," Charlie and Deb said together.

"I din know they did why slave in Messico Cidy."

"Oh, yes," Deb said. "The whitest."

"We met in a museum," Charlie said.

"We met in a park," Deb said.

They looked at each other.

Nan and Willy laughed.

"I don think they med ad all," Willy said.

"The Chapultepec Museum," Charlie said.

"In Chapultepec Park," Deb said.

"On the steps, outside it."

"I was in two minds," Deb said.

"She was at a crisis point in her life," Charlie said.

"I had to decide, you see."

"I see," Willy drawled. "Whether to go in and see the—the—the museum thingies."

"He's always had a gift with words," Nan said.

"I had to decide," Deb said, "whether to go north or south. It was a decision which I knew would affect my life."

"She had this friend," Charlie said magnanimously.

"I found a frien' today," Willy said. "A manager." He suddenly began to feel less frivolous.

"He was a minister," Deb said.

"What kind?" Nan asked.

"Public affairs and misinformation," Charlie said.

"Of a country. In the south. And he was fond of me. And I had to decide whether I was fond of him."

"And then you met Charlie," Nan said wistfully. "Oh, that's lovely. Why don't you ever put something lovely like that in your books, Willy?"

"He doesn't write that kind of book," Charlie said, defending his brother. "He writes about tough things, maybe not realistic things, maybe not sensitive things that people like Deb appreciate, but tough things."

Willy rubbed his head. He didn't know whether he was being defended or not. Or if he was, whether he needed to defend himself against the defense.

"Besides," Deb said, "it wasn't all that lovely. Not at first."

"Now, you don't need—" Charlie began.

"Charles thought I was a whore and I thought he was a junkie."

"You never told me you thought I was a junkie."

"Long sleeves in the summer?" Deb said. "How did I know then you were a long-sleeve fetishist?"

Charlie displayed his current long sleeves.

To his astonishment, Willy then caught sight of Boo Brinker across the room. She was on the arm of the silver-haired Barry Youngman and they were being shown to a table beside a sycamore in an alcove along a wall opposite.

At his own table everyone noticed Willy go rigid, but they thought at first he was making some kind of obscure jest.

"He's had too much to drink," Nan said. "He's been working a lot lately and he's not so used to socializing as he was."

Boo saw Willy almost immediately after she'd been seated, and she rose to come over to Willy's table.

As she approached, the party went silent.

"Willy" Boo said. She patted him extravagantly on the shoulder. "What a surprise to see you here, what a lovely surprise!"

"Hello," Willy said. He smiled stupidly.

"I'm with a friend or I would invite you all over. I kind of think we'll be talking about private things, you know?" She winked broadly. "Hey, there is the funniest thing. I found one of your credit cards. In the grass in front of our house. What about that! Isn't that weird?"

"Yes, weird," Willy managed to say.

"I'd have brought it along, only I didn't know you would be here. And if it comes to that, I didn't know I would be here. But I'm glad to see you 'cause I was thinking about what I said last time we talked, and I was afraid you might have took it the wrong way and I don't want that. You come around and let me straighten it out, O.K.? Or maybe I should come to your place for a change, if your wife wouldn't mind." She looked from Nan to Deb. "Which one is it, the icy one or the efficient one? Or have I made a little oopsie? Let me assure you, as far as I know, ladies, he doesn't have a wife."

"I am Nan," Nan said.

"Hi. I think I better go before I get Willy here into more trouble. Besides, I think Sweetie may be getting restless. Bye, now."

Boo swept away.

Everyone at the table looked at Willy.

But no one spoke until Deb, squinting in Boo's direction, asked, "Who is that young lady with? Her father?"

"Her father is dead," Willy said. "Murdered."

"Ahhh," Charlie said. He, too, looked toward Boo's table. "So that must be Miss Brinker."

"And the man she's with," Willy said, "is a salesman who worked for her late father."

"He's pretty old to be her boyfriend, isn't he?" Charlie asked.

"No man is ever too old to be a woman's boyfriend," Deb said.

"I don't know about that," Willy said. "And I didn't know they knew each other. But I do know that he lied to me."

"Lied to you?" Charlie asked.

"About a trailer. It's . . . it's a long story."

"Please do not tell it," Nan said. Firmly. Willy didn't speak.

"You have a responsibility to your brother not to spoil this lovely time. It is their anniversary, you know."

Willy felt trapped and conceded the point. He struggled to be lighthearted through the rest of the evening. But he stopped drinking and could not but notice that Youngman and Boo seemed to be getting along very well.

"Why didn't you tell me that Barbara Brinker had become a ravishing beauty," Nan demanded when finally they were home alone.

"Has she?"

"Don't play simple with me, William. And don't expect me to be pleased when you spend the bulk of the evening undressing her from across the room. I can't remember when I've been so embarrassed."

"I was not undressing her!"

"She was a pretty enough little thing at school," Nan said, "but I'd never have guessed she'd turn out like that."

"She's not all that . . . like that," Willy protested.

"And now defending her." Nan turned on him. "I thought there was something funny about your distraction with this so-called case. I understand what the attraction is now, though I must say I thought your tastes might be a little bit more refined."

"Oh, for Christ—"

"And what's that about your credit card in the grass? I thought in the grass was usually free."

"Don't be—"

"And now that it is clear the lady has other interests, perhaps we'll be seeing a bit more work out of you."

"I have been working," Willy protested again.

"Hmm. I wonder why. It couldn't be the weight of bills or contracts to fulfill or anything trivial like that."

"Oh, leave me alone."

"That's exactly what I intend to do."

Nan went upstairs.

Willy sat in the living room. Eventually he dozed on the couch for a few hours. But about dawn he got up, made himself coffee and went to work.

26

I parked the Doodah in McKeand's driveway. His house was in North Crow's Nest. It was big and had two protruding wings.

"Should we be out visible like this?" Mossman asked. "Won't he see the car if he comes here?"

"When he comes here."

"When."

"Sure he will. And good if he does. He saw it last outside McKeand's restaurant. It's too classy a vehicle for him to think a dumb private detective would own it."

"And are you a dumb private detective?"

"To him."

She smiled. She had a nice smile.

"You have a nice smile," I said.

"That's the second sweet thing you've said to me since we've met," she said. "If you hadn't punched me in the face, I'd think you were a softie."

"I am," I said. "A tough softie."

"I believe you."

"I don't trust people easily, which is what's kept me alive this long. But after I give someone the seal of approval, I'm putty in their hands. I stop hitting them. I compliment their smiles. There are no limits to my gestures of support."

"And you approve of me now, do you?"

I thought about it. "Yes."

"Good," she said.

"You've come through the last few hours pretty well and you don't seem afraid of what's coming up now."

She thought about what was coming up.

Instead of spelling it out, I asked, "How the hell did you get into this business? It's the only thing left that bothers me."

"Well, it happened by accident."

"Most of us do. But you're a cut above the other

lady private dicks I've come across."

"Compliment after compliment. I'm getting suspicious that you're after my virtue or something."

"I am," I said. "But not your virtue."

She paused and seemed to think. Then she put a hand on my cheek. It rested lightly there for several seconds and we looked at each other eye to eye. Her hand was soft and light and cool.

"You know," I said, "you are ravishingly beautiful."

"Jolly decent of you to notice at last," she said.

I began to unbutton her blouse. "You still haven't answered my question."

"Which question?" She began to unbutton my shirt.

"How you got into this line of work."

She raised an eyebrow. I raised something to match.

"Was it through work with some kind of security company?" I slipped the blouse back over her shoulders and down her arms. Her skin was smooth and warm to the touch, downy in the valleys.

"No," she said. She eased my shirt and jacket off and pulled gently at the hair on my chest.

"Or were you with the police?" Her skirt had a catch at the side and a short zipper; her bra hooked between the cups.

"No." My pants had buttons at the front. I don't wear a belt or a bra.

"Or maybe you were in the army, in intelligence."

"No," she said.

The Doodah did one of its tricks, with the seats, and I lowered her gently beside me. Her warmth penetrated to my core, where I was already pretty warm.

"How then?" I asked.

"How...how what?"

"How did a nice girl like you—?"

"Become a private inquiry agent? Oh. Oh . . . I . . . I started in the movies."

"The movies?"

"That's right. I was in a few lightly pornographic films after I left home."

"I can just see you in a skin flick," I said.

"But I didn't seem to have the aptitude for it."

"I find that hard to believe," I said.

"I didn't come across on film," she said.

"Oh," I said. "Ah. Where did you come across?"

"Then I had a friend....He was an inquiry agent and he got me involved. Oh."

"Got you involved."

"That's right."

"With detection?"

"And then I..."

"You."

"Set up..."

"Yes?"

"On my..."

"Yes, yes?"

"Own."

"Oh, yes?"

"Yes!"

"Yes!"

27

"You were up early," Nan said when she came down.

"I was working."

"So I heard," she said.

"Sorry," Willy said formally. "There's coffee in the pot."

Nan poured a cup and then turned to him.

He was instantly aware of this sudden move, but she said, "Did I give you your letter?"

"What letter?"

"There was a letter yesterday morning for you."

"I never saw it."

Nan looked for and found the envelope. "With all the things happening, I forgot about it."

Willy took the envelope and studied it. It was from Terre Haute. He frowned, then opened it.

"I'm sorry if I was nasty last night," Nan said.

"Mmm."

"Willy?"

"Look at this," he said. "Look at this!" He waved the letter. "They're canceling me!"

"They're not publishing your book?" Nan was shocked.

"No. Don't be silly. It's the Terre Haute Writers' Circle. 'Due to a sharp drop in our membership we are forced to contract our anticipated program for the current season.'"

"Oh, is that all?"

"All? It's too much! I was ready for them."

"When were you supposed to go?"

"May sometime."

"How can you have been ready?"

"I did some thinking about it. Getting my lines ready. About how Hank is just a narrative device; about how he is and is not me at the same time; about how I would be glad to autograph copies of my book for them but wouldn't they prefer to have the rare copies, the unautographed ones."

"Narrative device?" Nan said with the slightest of questioning in her tone.

"You see fictional detectives aren't people," Willy began.

"That's all right, you don't—"

"They are only excuses for the authorial point of view to intrude into—"

"All right! I remember, I remember."

Willy stopped. "Another fat fee down the drain."

"How much was it?"

"I asked for forty bucks plus expenses."

"Asked for?"

"They didn't mention money in the first letter, so I wrote back and asked for forty. They can't expect to get quality for nothing."

"You could offer to go anyway."

"In a pig's ear," he said. "But why don't you take my place, seeing as you have all my little glibnesses off pat anyway."

Nan didn't answer.

"Hey, that's not a bad idea," Willy continued, weariness blurring his wariness. "They'd find it quite interesting that instead of just writing under a pen name you also write under a pen sex."

Nan did not find it so interesting.

"When people ask me what name I write under because they've never heard of me, I think about saying 'Agatha Christie' but I've never quite had the nerve."

"There's still time!" Nan said. "You're not dead yet."

"True, true."

"You seem pretty sprightly, considering the state you were in last night." Acidly.

"Can't feel rotten all the time," Willy said. "I mean what are little things like hangovers and no sleep? Trifles."

Nan asked, "Are you working again this morning?"

Willy decided the question was hostile. "For crying out loud, you're trying to wring blood out of me now."

"There's no need to shout. I only asked."

"I didn't shout."

"You did, but I don't want to fight about it."

"Why did you ask whether I was working again?"

"I just thought you might not be."

Willy felt offended that she was nagging him again. "It's not your business anyway," he said.

With self-control Nan said, "No need to get ruffled. I only asked."

"I only answered," Willy said.

Nan said nothing.

"How many times do I have to tell you," Willy said, "that everything I do is related to my work? If I'm thinking about something—"

"Oh, shut up!" Nan shouted. "I'm not your Writers' Circle!"

"What does that have to do with the price of gas?"

She stood in front of him. "I asked whether you intended to work because I thought if you were tired you might want to go back to bed. If you were going back to bed, I wasn't going to vacuum or turn on the radio."

"Don't do me any favors."

"Honestly, Willy, you are beyond talking to."

He said, "Here I was in a perfectly good mood and you have to go and bomb it."

"Me! You're outrageous! You're the one making trouble out of nothing. And you feel entitled because you feel pleased with yourself for having done some work before breakfast. Don't work any more today, I don't care. Go out and solve the Brinker murder if you want to. Solve a mugging and a case of child abuse for good measure if you're in the mood, I don't give a damn. If I go out of my way to fit in with your work when you're under pressure, it's only because I find it hard not to try to help. But go do whatever the hell you want to. Sleep all day under the shower if you want to, but don't you accuse me of starting trouble this morning, because that's just not how things happened."

Nan stormed out of the kitchen.

Not to be left out of the general effect and tone, Willy stormed out of the house. He got into his car and drove away, fast. After he had been driving for a few minutes, he realized he was heading for Castleton.

As he approached the Brinkers' house, Willy wondered if he should have called to warn Boo he was coming. He considered turning around to find a phone. But she had asked him to come out, to clarify whether she wanted him to keep working on the case, so Willy let it ride.

However, when Willy rang the doorbell, it was Lorraine Brinker who opened the door.

"Oh, Willy! Thank heavens!" She grabbed him and pulled him inside. "How did you know? How did you know?" She drew him not to the living room but into the kitchen. Once there, she sat on a chair and began to sob, saying, "Boo didn't come home last night. She went out and she hasn't come back. My God, it's just like Larry. It's happening all over again. I don't think I can bear it. I don't think I can bear it!"

She jumped off of the chair and pushed herself onto his chest. She pulled at his shirt. Willy held her, patted her on the back, tried to comfort her as he would comfort Nan.

In response she put her arms around him and before long her sobbing stopped.

Willy stood.

After several seconds, Lorraine Brinker suddenly took her arms from around him and pushed him sharply away. Willy released her immediately and she turned her back to him.

Willy had a shocked moment when he wondered if she was taking what had happened as his having made a pass at her.

But she took a deep breath and faced him, flushed, and her eyes bright. "She's usually very good, you know," she said.

"What?"

"When she was a girl, if she was going to be late home, she was very good about calling to tell us."

"Oh," Willy said.

"It didn't seem very satisfactory then, but I would have given a lot for a call from her last night." Matter-of-factly, Lorraine Brinker wiped her hands over her cheeks and continued the movement to brush back through her hair.

Willy was about to say that he'd seen Boo the previous night, but Lorraine Brinker said, "She went out in the afternoon yesterday. After the funeral. She said she was going to play tennis."

"That's all she said she was doing?" Willy asked. He was somewhat shocked.

"Yes." She began to sniffle again.

"And you expected her back for dinner?"

"Well, she hasn't been eating here much."

"Where has she been eating?"

"Out. Oh, I don't know. Why do you cross-examine me like this, Willy Werth? What are you trying to do? Prove that I'm a bad mother because I don't know where my daughter goes when she goes out? I'll trouble you to remind yourself that she's nineteen and has been a law unto herself for a long time now. It's not my responsibility where she is or what she does."

"I'm sorry," Willy said. He felt oppressed by lack of transition. "It's just that—" he began.

"I know. It's not your problem. But I do worry."

"Of course you should worry. But last night Nan and I went out to dinner with my brother and his wife—"

Lorraine Brinker jumped back as if she had been shot. "But I thought you were trying to find out who killed Larry," she said.

"I am."

"But . . . But . . ." Then, "I didn't realize it was only a part-time thing for you," she said plaintively. "I thought you were—" She caught her breath and at the same time slapped her own hand. "Foolish me," she said. "How could I possibly think that you could take it so seriously?"

"I do take it seriously," Willy said with immediate feeling. "I couldn't help having to go out last night."

"Of course not. And you have your own work and interests and a million other commitments."

Willy felt uneasy. "I was only trying to say that while I was out last night I saw Boo."

Her eyes wide, Lorraine Brinker said softly. "You saw Barbara?"

"Yes. She was eating at the same place we were."

"Alone?"

"No."

"How stupid can I be?" Lorraine Brinker said. "Boo wouldn't eat alone. Not her. Not like me for the rest of my life."

"She was with one of Larry's salesmen. Barry Youngman."

"My God!" Lorraine Brinker said. "Him?"

"You know him?"

"But he's so old," she said.

"You've met him?"

"A few times. He always makes me uncomfortable. He seems so . . . so opportunistic. Larry thought so, too."

"He didn't get along with Larry?"

"You keep questioning me, Willy. Why do you keep questioning me?"

It suddenly struck Willy, sharply, that because of his own personal convenience—work, guests—and his pique with Hearns, he had been keeping to himself the information that might be relevant to Larry Brinker's murder. Information about Barry Youngman. Willy felt a wave of guilt at his irresponsibility. Hank wouldn't have let life get in the way of duty; neither would Hearns. The wave became a tide. "I'm sorry," Willy said. "But I'm thinking about having seen Boo with Youngman, and about where one should start to look for her."

"Oh, Willy, would you look for her? Would you? Oh, thank you, Willy!"

"I . . ." He was committed.

"She's not really in danger, I'm sure. It's all just a coincidence, but it would be a great weight off my mind. I'd be terribly grateful, I really would."

"I'll . . . I'll do what I can," he said.

"She only told me she was going to play tennis," Lorraine Brinker said. "I don't like to ask her questions, because you have to show faith in your child, don't you?"

Willy frowned. Preoccupied with coincidences, and with his racing heart.

"Don't make that face. You'll make me think it's all going to happen again. And that's silly. Of course it's silly."

Taking the cue, Willy said, "But it's just as well to track her down, to know where she is, even if there's nothing to worry about."

"That's right," Lorraine Brinker said.

Willy rose to leave.

"She's a good girl," Lorraine Brinker said again as she followed Willy to the door. "Really she is. Very moral, underneath. But I just wish she'd find somebody her own age, you know what I mean?"

As Willy walked down the steps from the front porch, he heard her muttering, "How can she do this to me! At a time like this!"

Willy didn't know. If she'd last been seen with anyone besides Youngman . . .

Willy pulled away from the house immediately, but as soon as he was out of sight he parked again, to think.

But thinking only fed the agitation he felt rising within. When he started the motor again, he felt frightened.

In police headquarters Willy took the elevator to the fourth floor and presented himself to the reception officer at Homicide and Robbery with Violence. He asked for Hearns, but before Hearns could be called, he appeared. Hearns entered the office, in a hurry, from the Detective Day Room. At the same time, a morose-looking man in a gray suit entered from the corridor.

When he saw Willy, Hearns stopped and said, "Well, look who's here." He took the man in the gray suit by the arm. "Look who's here, Lieutenant!"

The man stopped and stared gloomily at Willy.

"It's William Werth, the famous writer," Hearns said. "You've heard of him. He writes the Hank Midwinter books. Hank Midwinter is a giant among pygmies in the world of Indianapolis private detectives."

"There's no need to be snide," Willy said.

"Don't underrate yourself, Mr. Werth."

The lieutenant pulled free from Hearns and continued on his way.

"You're wasting time," Willy said urgently.

"The hell you say," Hearns said, concentrating on Willy again. "Who is wasting whose time?"

"The Brinkers' daughter has gone missing."

"Go find her then." Hearns pushed past Willy and left the office.

Willy pursued him into the corridor where Hearns now stood in front of the elevator. "You don't understand. She's been gone all night, and when I last saw her she—"

Hearns took Willy by the lapels of his jacket, which shocked Willy into silence. With the appearance of great effort at self-control, Hearns said, "I'm glad you're here, Mr. Werth."

"What?"

"I have been meaning to call you. I wanted to apologize for my outburst in your house."

"You did?"

"It wasn't polite, but it happened because I hate people who are sensationalizing parasites on the kind of dirty things that I am paid to clean up. But I've checked you out, and people tell me you have not made a career of exploiting situations like this one. So I am sorry I was uncontrolled with you."

"I—" Willy began to say that he was only trying to help.

"However, it remains unaltered that I do not want or need your assistance. You say Miss Brinker is missing? Go back into the office and ask the officer to direct you to Missing Persons. We have a fella there who will deal with you, enthusiastically, and if I wasn't on my way to do something important, I'd take you to him myself just so I could watch. But

I am leaving now. And I don't have time to talk to you anymore. Goodbye, Mr. Werth."

As if on cue, elevator doors opened before them. Hearns let Willy go and stepped into the elevator. Willy took a step after him, but as if he had seen, Hearns whirled and pointed a finger and said, "Stay. Keep back. I will go down in this elevator alone. If you make one more move to follow me, I'll have you locked up."

Hearns kept pointing his finger as long as Willy could see him.

Back in the parking lot, Willy sat in his car. He felt himself becoming more and more agitated. He wanted to think, to be thorough, calm and incisive.

His conscious mind, the words he talked to himself with, argued that anxiety was absurd, that Boo was irresponsible but safe. Able to take care of herself. But battling against the dread of Boo being unaccounted for, against his feeling about Youngman's dangerousness, against his sense of having himself acted irresponsibly, the words carried little sway.

Willy started the car and hit the accelerator.

Youngman's phone-book address was on Kentucky Avenue. Although it seemed unlikely Youngman would be there, it was nearer downtown than the Brinker's Mobile Homes site. And as far as Willy's fears were concerned, finding Youngman would be the next best thing to finding Boo.

The number was not a house, however, but a liquor store. Willy parked and went in. There were no customers, but stepping on the mat inside the door triggered a bell and brought an old man in a red jacket from a back room. He had an oval face, crusted top and bottom with white hair, and moved quickly despite his years.

"Can I help you?" he asked in a firm voice.

"I'm looking for Barry Youngman," Willy said baldly.

"I'm Barry Youngman," the man said. "What can I do you for?"

Willy was momentarily speechless with surprise.

But if Willy hadn't expected the situation, the old man had. "You're not looking for me then. You want my son."

"Ah, yes," Willy said.

"What kind of goddamn bill collector are you?"

"I'm not," Willy said.

"Makes a change," the old man said. "Ever since he moved in here again, I had a stream of guys come in looking for money he owes. If they each bought a bottle of bourbon, I'd have made enough to pay them off." He chuckled at the idea. "You want a bottle of bourbon?"

"No, thanks," Willy said. "Your son's not here, that right?"

"That's right all right. I haven't seen him since yesterday."

"He didn't come home last night?"

"No."

"Is that something he does a lot?"

"He stays over with a pal from work from time to time. Leastways that's what he tells me." The old man wagged his head from side to side. "But I reckon there's things he thinks a son shouldn't tell his father." He chuckled again.

Willy asked, "And you say he's in debt."

"That's usually the story when you go bankrupt," the old man said sternly. "Half the reason I keep alive is so he won't get out of his own trouble easy, with my money."

"So he wouldn't usually go out to eat in fancy restaurants?"

"Like where?"

"The Sycamores?"

"Son of a bitch!"

As Willy left, Barry Youngman, Sr., said, "But the other half of the reason I keep alive is there's things that I reckon a father shouldn't tell a son."

It was with increasingly raw fear that Willy pulled sharply into the ex-motel where Sam Shilton lived. He parked in front of Shilton's door and knocked. There was no answer and he knocked again. And again. He tested the door. It was locked but the frame seemed to yield a little when he pushed. He pushed again.

"What you doing, mister?"

Willy turned to face a man who stood behind him leaning heavily on a cane.

"What's all the noise about?"

"I'm looking for the man who lives here."

"Sammy'd be at work," the man said.

"Did another man stay over here last night?"

"Dunno about that, mister. But Sammy ain't here and I know that same as I know I'll live again in Heaven."

"O.K.," Willy said.

"And same as I know you shouldn't push at a man's door if nobody comes when you pound on it loud enough to wake the dead."

As if his worst fears had only to be understood to be confirmed, Willy found police cars blocking the entrance to Brinker's Mobile Homes. Five or six people stood around outside the premises with two uniformed policemen in full view just inside the gate.

Willy parked on Washington Street and ran back to the crowd.

The first person he came to was an elderly woman with a shopping bag. "What's happened?" he asked her, short of breath. "What's happened?"

Aware Willy had been running to get there just to ask this question, she said, "Don't ask me." But less implying ignorance than wanting nothing to do with a lunatic.

A teenage boy turned to Willy and said, "Cops are here."

"I can see that. Why?"

"I think they come to arrest somebody for murder."

"My God! My God!" Willy said. He felt the panic of an event that was horrible and irretrievable.

"Don't get so excited," the boy said. "It happens every day."

"Are you absolutely certain she's dead?" Willy asked.

"What she?" the boy asked. "All I know is the guy that owned this place got bumped off last week."

"His daughter," Willy said. "Is his daughter all right?"

"I don't know about no daughter."

"Has there been an ambulance?"

"I ain't seen one, but I ain't been here very long," the boy said. "And all I know is I think they come in to arrest one of the salesmen."

"What the hell makes you so informed about it?" asked the old woman. She waved her shopping bag at the boy. "You shouldn't tell tales. Don't they teach you anything about honorable behavior in schools these days?"

"Fuck you, lady," the boy said. "I know," he confided to Willy, "because I was in the office when the cops rolled up. I deliver doughnuts and coffee. I'm at Tastee Coffy down the road there, you know it?"

"Fuck yourself," the old lady said. She walked away.

"And I brought over the coffee and stuff they usually have, see. And then the cops blew in."

"What did they say?" Willy asked urgently.

"They told me to get lost is what," the boy said. He turned to look past the cars toward the business office. "I hope they hurry. I can't hang around much longer. I want to find out what happens but I need the job, you know?" The boy looked at his watch. He shifted his jaw uneasily.

"Well, did they mention a girl?" Willy asked.

The boy shook his head.

"Who exactly was in there?"

"Just the two salesmen, Shifty Sam and Hairy Barry. No girls. It's not about girls, you know, mister."

"Barry Youngman is in there?"

"Yeah."

"You're sure?"

"Sure I'm sure. I know Hairy Barry when I see him."

"Thanks," Willy said. He pushed past the boy and between the cars.

A large patrolman moved sharply into his path. "Get your ass back on the sidewalk, you."

"It's all right, Officer," Willy said. "I represent the family." He tried to walk past the policeman. He found himself restrained efficiently and none too gently by a substantial arm.

"Nice try, buddy."

"No, it's O.K., really," Willy said.

"What family is you supposed to represent? The Mafia?"

"The Brinkers," Willy said. "The family that owns this place. The man who was murdered."

The policeman asked, "Lawyer?"

Willy almost said "Private detective" but instead just repeated, "A representative. I represent Mrs. Brinker and her daughter."

"Ahhh, a reporter."

"No, no. Look, I've got papers in my pocket and they know me in there."

"Hearns knows you?"

The name made Willy cautious, but, "Yeah. Hearns knows me."

The policeman looked at Willy steadily for a moment. Then shrugged. "What's your name?"

Willy told him.

"Stay here."

The policeman called over his colleague and said, "This guy says Hearns knows him. I'm gonna go ask. He's O.K. staying here."

The other patrolman nodded and Willy's man started toward the business office.

He'd taken three steps when the door to the office flew open. A furious Hearns marched out. Behind him four other men followed: Barry Youngman, Sam Shilton and two uniformed policemen.

Willy's policemen stood still as Hearns drew near.

Hearns said, "Clear those gawkers out of there. There's nothing to see." He waved a finger in the general direction of the onlookers.

Willy ran toward Hearns. "What about Barbara Brinker, the Brinkers' daughter? Have you found her yet?"

Hearns noticed Willy for the first time. "And get that idiot the hell out of my way!" he shouted.

Sharply the patrolman Willy had talked to pulled Willy aside. "He knows you all right," he said under his breath.

Hearns watched as the other four men piled into one of the police cars. Then he turned to the tiny crowd and shouted, "That's all! It's all over! Get out of the way of the cars and get back to the business you've been neglecting while you've been rubbernecking here." The police car pulled out.

To the patrolmen he said, "Get the lady that owns this place on the phone and tell her to get somebody to lock the joint up. When somebody comes, clear off."

"Yes, sir."

Hearns got into a car himself, started it and squealed onto West Washington Street, heading for town.

The patrolman holding Willy let him go. "I guess the world's safe from you now." He didn't wait for a reply. "Hey, Rat Face, what do we do now?"

"Call the owner like the man said."

"Do you know the number?"

"Hell no. I only work here."

Willy's cop turned to him. "Are you really something to do with the family or was that just a line?"

Willy gave them Lorraine Brinker's telephone number. The cop Willy had talked to went into the office to call her while Rat Face stayed with Willy. "If it was me," he said confidingly, "I'd leave the place to you, if you're something to do with the family. But he's big on doing things by the book, my friend on the phone there. Nice guy, but he's got to loosen up, you know what I mean?"

Willy nodded. Then he asked the cop, "Was anything said about Brinker's daughter this morning?"

"Look, don't ask me about details. A call comes to assist, we assist. That's where it starts and that's where it ends. All I know is it looks like two guys are on their way downtown instead of spending their morning in the air-conditioned office."

Before long, the other policeman came back. He asked Willy, "Is that Mrs. Brinker a nut case or something?"

"What do you mean?"

"I call her about locking the place up here, and all she wants to go on about is how some guy is after her daughter. Is that you?"

"I'm trying to find her, yes."

"Is she lost?"

"Missing."

"Yeah?" Both policemen perked up. "Since when?"

"Yesterday," Willy said.

"Oh, well," Rat Face said.

"Is this a little kid?" the more earnest cop asked.

"Nineteen."

"Oh hell."

"So what did she say about this place?" Rat Face asked.

"Oh, she said she's quite happy to leave it all to our friend here."

"Good," Rat Face said. "Let's split." They walked to their cars.

Willy stood in the gateway and watched them drive away.

He felt anxious and also absurd.

The relative mildness of the morning was passing, to unleash the heat of the day. Willy felt unable to think effectively. He decided to walk around the lot for a while.

As he walked he tried to relax, aware that the underpinning

of anxiety still kept him from being able to sort out priorities, to make plans.

He took deep breaths. As he walked past the trailers, he started counting them. Gradually, he became mildly interested in differences between them, in what made them more and less mobile, less and more homes.

The only time he'd had any substantial excess of money, the time of the movie of *Hayride Horror,* he'd used the surplus to buy an immobile home. But he now thought about having one of these units, a little one. To use as an office, perhaps. A secondary office, to get away in when he was having trouble working in the office in the house. Not a bad idea.

Willy started looking in the windows of the trailers.

If he didn't alter the inside too much, he and Nan could use it for vacations as well. A possible idea. Possible.

Problems, though. Taxes, for one. How much would be deductible if the place were not for the sole purposes of work? Might be problems there. He didn't know the prices, either.

Then he thought it not impossible that Lorraine Brinker would give him a trailer, a small used one, for services rendered. At least she'd give him a good price on one.

Or Boo would, if she was doing the business side.

Boo. Oh Christ!

Willy held his hand over his mouth as Boo came back into his mind, as if he had spoken evil of the dead.

Then he realized that he was at the trailer Larry Brinker's body had been found in.

He stood outside it without moving.

He shook his head to clear it.

He looked in an end window where the Venetian blinds had not been completely closed.

Nothing. A kitchen.

He shrugged, walked along the side and then noticed a window with the curtains partly open. He looked in.

In the dim interior he saw Boo Brinker. She was sprawled awkwardly on a bed. Naked except for a splash of red across her neck and on the bed.

Willy jumped back.

"Oh!" he said, choked, barely aloud. It felt like a scream.

He couldn't believe he'd seen what he'd seen.

He stepped to the window again, conscious now of the

lacelike netting covering the window in addition to the curtain.

For a moment he thought there was nothing in the trailer after all.

But there was.

It was Boo. Still. As before.

The scream came out clear and loud this time. "Ahhhhhhhhh!"

Willy stepped jerkily back.

He stood for several seconds shaking all over.

He fell to one knee.

He threw up.

Then, in front of him, the trailer door opened and Boo Brinker asked, "What's all the racket?"

Willy sat on a stool while Boo made him a cup of coffee.

"There," she said, putting the cup and saucer on an eating shelf beside him, "get that down and you'll feel better."

Willy said, "I thought you were dead."

"Me!"

Willy nodded.

"I'm too young to die," Boo said.

Willy drank from the coffee.

"Gee," she said, "and you got all upset just because you thought that. You're a real nice man, Mr. Werth."

"You," Willy said, "in this trailer . . ." Only as he began to relax did he become aware again that she wore nothing but a blood-red scarf at her neck.

"Oh, the cops are finished with it. They gave me back the key."

"That's not what I meant."

"Well, what then?"

"Your . . . your . . ."

"Oh, you mean because of Dad." She paused for thought. "Well, something like that doesn't affect the place, does it? It's still just a trailer, after all. Metal and stuff."

Willy said nothing.

"So last night when the occasion arose"—a slight giggle—"it seemed the logical place. I mean I couldn't take him back home with me now, could I? So . . ." A shrug.

"Your mother was very upset," Willy said.

"It's none of her business."

"About your not coming home last night."

"I'm a big girl," Boo said. She rubbed herself, her ribs and stomach, and lingered over the process. Then she said, "I've often not come home all night."

"You have? . . . Haven't?"

"Sure. Before I split for New York, lots of times. I can't say they ever liked it much, my folks, my mom, but there wasn't much they could do about it."

"But since you've been back?"

"I haven't stayed out all night, no, but it's not the kind of thing you do by yourself, is it?" A big smile. "And she can't expect me to go on acting the dutiful daughter till I drop. Not the dutiful daughter staying at home to look after the widowed mother. I mean, it's just not the kind of part I am cast for. Shit, I've surprised myself by hanging around this long. This is a pretty dull burg, you know. Compared to New York."

Willy sipped his coffee and worked out that Boo had been in town less than a week. He felt increasingly calm.

"You could have called your mother," he said.

"I don't need her permission."

"To keep her from worrying."

"She'd worry anyway. That's what mothers are for."

"Still—" Willy began.

Boo giggled. "Besides, as things turned out, you know, there wasn't a lot of chance to get to the telephone."

"Not even this morning?"

"I was sleeping! You saw. I was sleeping, which, after the amount of sleep I didn't get last night, was about the only thing I could do."

"Don't you realize how much like your father being missing this was for her?"

Boo was hard. "She ought to know I might be late. She always knew before. She doesn't like it, but she ought to know and she should have just gone to sleep. She can't be treated delicately forever."

A week, Willy thought. Forever to a Boo, perhaps.

Willy pushed his coffee away and looked again around the trailer.

"It's just a place!" Boo said. "There's no such thing as ghosts. A place is just a place!"

"I wasn't thinking that," Willy said. Though he had been, of ghosts of the mind.

"Aw, come on, Mr. Werth," Boo said. She showed concern

at his disapproval. "I thought you liked me. Don't be mean just because I didn't call my goddamn mother and tell her I had better things to do than come home at ten and cuddle up with my teddy bear."

Willy said nothing, since he couldn't think of anything to say that was nice.

"Aw, come on, Willy," she said again. "Isn't there some way for us to make up and be friends again?" She tilted her head coyly. "After all, I am kind of at your mercy." A giggle. "And you like me, I know you do."

Willy said nothing, showed nothing.

Boo didn't like it. "Or is guys and chicks the sort of thing that only happens in your books?"

Willy got up and left the trailer.

As Willy arrived home, he looked for Nan's car but it wasn't there.

He wasn't surprised, but he was disappointed. He walked through to the living room and stood awhile, looking out the window, listening to house sounds. He realized he was listening for her.

He went to the kitchen, to the refrigerator, and opened the door. After looking at the shelves for a few moments he closed the door again. It was still early to eat.

He was sitting at the breakfast table when Nan's car came up the driveway.

Willy walked out to meet her, grinning. "You're back," he said as she got out of the car and turned to pull a box of groceries across the seat.

"I was shopping and wanted to get the frozen stuff away," she said. "It's so damn hot."

He took the box from her. She led him to the kitchen. "Anywhere," she said. "Next to the icebox."

She finally turned to look at him. "What's up with you, Willy Werth? Did you just catch a mouse?"

"Give me a kiss," he said.

"What?" But she stepped to him and kissed him lightly on the cheek. "Poor Willy," she said.

"Why poor?" he asked.

"You can't have been feeling very good about life lately."

"I'm all right. I just don't quite know what to do."

"It's not like you to be uncertain of life," she said.

"I suppose not."

"I've never known anyone like you for knowing your own mind."

"I guess."

"Just don't forget, I'm on your side."

"My side of what?"

"Don't be obstructive."

"O.K.," he said. "I get swept up."

"Don't fret."

"I want to take you to bed," he said.

"No you don't," Nan said.

"I don't?"

"You'd really rather work."

"I don't feel much like working."

"Yes you do," she said quietly.

28

We rested in The Doodah.

I began to get nervous. Mossman recognized it.

She asked, "Is there any chance that he might not come here after all?"

"None," I said, on the theory that I can do my worrying for myself.

"Aren't you ever wrong?"

"No."

She pulled away. "What's the matter with you?" she asked. "I'm on your side, remember. Or do you go off women after midnight?"

"I'm all right."

"Come on, now, indulge me." She was sounding wifely all of a sudden. Which felt unexpectedly pleasant.

"O.K.," I said. "I don't know whether he is coming or not."

She nodded.

"I get times," I said, "when I get so involved that I lose knowledge of whether I'm reacting correctly or not. Whether I'm responding to what's happening around me or what's happening inside me. I get swept up. And if I'm wrong, I just reason from mistake to mistake. I end up washed out with my own stupidities. I can't help feeling that my life is a bit unreal."

She rubbed my temples.

"I'm certain he's coming. But whether I'm right to be certain I don't know."

"You're not very used to being unsure," Mossman said.

"I don't get a lot of practice."

"It's not a bad thing," she said.

"A man should be hard and sure," I said.

"Only at the right time and in the right place."

"Is that by way of a suggestion?"

She never answered. Brock Hallett shot her
through The Doodah's window.

*   *   *

Production cars are for production people. Over the
years I have had The Doodah enhanced with a
number of specialist features. And while I cannot say
that I had ever anticipated being shot at in those
particular circumstances, the possibility of needing a
weapon when I wasn't wearing my shoulder holster
had been allowed for. I have a .38 S. & W. Airweight
installed on a spring clip. Only five shots and a
tendency to be inaccurate, but very light for a
revolver and good in a scramble.

Before he fired again, I had it in my hand.

And I shot first.

I didn't hit him, but glass flying out in front of a
flash surprised the hell out of him.

He'd shot Mossman instead of me because he'd
been certain of his control of the situation. Presuming
that without clothes I had to be unarmed.

He wasn't the stand-and-fight type. But he had the
presence of mind to shoot out my closest tire as he
turned tail and hared for the cover of the house.

Mossman was still breathing. A resilient item. I
piled clothes onto where the blood was coming out of
her.

I had to decide whether to go on a three-wheeled
excursion looking for help or to go into the house to
use the telephone and bring the help to her.

There was no real choice. I slipped out of The
Doodah and followed shadows to the house.

The front door was locked. Hallett had gone around
the back. I smashed the closest window, cleared the
jagged edges and clambered in, missing, as best I
could, the sharp bits on the floor. Most of them.

I only had four bullets left, though he didn't know
that. I wondered whether he knew more about the
layout inside the house than I did.

He couldn't have known less. What light had been
provided by moon and stars outside was missing here.

I had the sense that I was in a big space, but I couldn't see anything.

The floor was bare and cool under my feet. Smooth stone.

I keep a penlight in my jacket pocket, but the only pockets available to me now were pockets of the flesh.

I knew I had to get out of wherever I was.

I started walking in the darkness.

After five steps I hit something. It was tall, thin and cold.

No, I haven't met your wife.

I felt it. It was a statue, in the middle of the floor. I became aware in the room of a number of other columns of vague whiteness. The place was filled with statues! And busts, no doubt, on pedestals.

The one I ran into had a hand out. With something in it, like an apple.

I wasn't hungry, but I broke it off. With only four bullets, something to throw might come in handy.

Just about that time a light came on behind me.

29

"You look pale, Willy," Nan said as he came into the kitchen. "Are you all right? Do you want some iced tea?"

"Yeah," he said. He sat down. "I'm fine."

"How did it go?"

"It's O.K.," he said. "I enjoyed it. I've got Hank, naked—apart from his gun—being stalked in a mansion full of statues."

"Naked?" She laughed.

"He was interrupted while his guard was down," Willy said. "See, the villain shot his girl friend and Hank is chasing after him."

"Hank's not going to club him to death with part of his anatomy, is he?"

"Good idea," Willy said.

Nan gave him the tea.

Willy said, "I've got this image of Hank chasing someone through a field of statues throwing hand grenades. There's a kind of sublime-ridiculous interface there. Great art and great destruction. Only I haven't quite managed to get him the grenades or the field."

"Did your vision have Hank without any clothes on?"

"That kind of came out of the situation."

"Hank always did travel light," Nan said.

Willy sipped his tea.

"How does the ignoble savage get out of it then?"

"After an exchange of gunfire, Hank will throw this piece of stone at him. It will hit the guy in the head, and while he's dazed Hank will jump him and bash him to death on the floor."

"Charming."

"Mmm, I like it, too," Willy said.

"But," Nan said, "I thought you said all Hank has is his gun."

"Oh, he breaks a piece off one of the statues."

"Off a statue! Oh, Willy—"

"It's perfectly possible if the marble isn't too thick."

"But it's so gross. I mean if they are meant to be art . . ."

Willy said, "It's something Hank would do. In the situation."

"Well," Nan said, "maybe Hank would."

"Tomorrow I'll go back and make him feel a moment of
remorse."

"That will make it all right then," Nan said.

"After all, he's revenging the lady he loves."

Nan was surprised. "He loves this one? I thought he never
loved them."

"This one's special."

"Willy?"

"Yeah?"

"You said she was shot."

"That's right."

"Does she die?"

"I've been worrying about that," Willy said. "The original
idea was that she was different for him, and then she had her
head blown off and that made Hank so mad that he tore after
the guy and made hamburger out of him. But when it came
to it, I couldn't actually pull her plug. She's still breathing at
the moment. I'll decide the next day or two."

"I'm glad she's still breathing."

"I'd like her to live, but it makes technical problems if she
isn't killed outright."

"Oh," Nan said.

"See, he really likes her."

"Hank likes them all," Nan said.

"But she's special. I always intended her to be special,
because I planned to bump her off. But if I don't bump her
off..."

"They could go into business together."

He reflected. "Hmm. She is a private detective."

"Well, there you are."

"But she would be bound to cramp his style."

"The way wives do," Nan said.

"Ahhh," Willy said. "That's it."

"What?"

"I could give her a husband. As she regains consciousness,
with Hank at her bedside, she calls out 'Throckmorton,' and
Hank knows that he will never come first. 'Who is Throckmorton?' he asks her. 'My husband,' she says. 'I never knew
you had a husband,' he says. 'You never asked,' she says."

"Didn't he ask?"

"Nope."

"That was a bit careless, wasn't it?"

"Hank never asks. Hank isn't afraid of husbands."

Nan stood and looked at him.

"What's wrong?" he asked.

"Nothing," she said. "It's just nice to talk to you again."

He sipped his tea.

"I feel better," Willy said.

"I've gathered that," Nan said, then hesitated. "You have heard the news, haven't you?"

"About what?"

She waited to decide whether he was serious, then understood that he was. She looked at her watch. "Turn the TV on in a few minutes," she said. "I'm hot. I'm going up to take a shower."

Willy sipped from his tea while the lunchtime television news worked its way to the story of the arrest of Neil Tudge, The Kid, for the murder of Larry Brinker.

Tudge, nineteen, had used the Brinker business's delivery of trailers to transport stolen goods for his older brother. The goods involved were cigarettes, liquor and electrical appliances. The shipments had been occasional, but of considerable value, and the police were investigating the possible connection of the older Tudge with other criminal elements. The older brother was also in custody.

On the night of the shooting, Brinker had apparently confronted young Tudge with a gun after coming to investigate sounds that had aroused his suspicion. There had been a fight, during which the gun had discharged, killing Brinker instantly. Tudge had moved the body into a trailer to try to disguise what had happened.

The other salesmen from the business were giving the police considerable assistance in reconstructing the scope and nature of Tudge's activities.

When Nan came down, Willy was sitting in front of the picture window, watching the street.

"You heard?" she asked.

He turned and smiled. "I heard."

"I had the radio on before I went shopping," she said. "I thought maybe you were there. That you were involved."

"I was there," Willy said. "But I wasn't involved. I wasn't close. I wasn't even warm."

"Oh," she said. Then, "Well, what would you like to do? Do you want to go out later? A movie or something?"

Instead of answering, Willy said, "I've been sitting here thinking where Hank is going next. The next book."

"He's not going abroad again, is he? You're not going to send him to England after that girl, are you?"

"Naw," Willy said. "Hank's too strong to let himself get preoccupied by something like love. No, I'm going to trap him. In town."

"In . . ."

"In Indianapolis. Downtown. Kind of the opposite of sending him traveling. I'll put him in a situation where he can't get out of someplace downtown. Total restriction, which permeates to the center of his being. Like being caught in a terrible blizzard or something. Or maybe not a blizzard. What about a huge flood from White River? What do you think?"

"Seriously?"

"Yeah. What do you think?"

"I think you better go upstairs and finish this one before you put too much energy into the next one. That's what I think."

Willy went upstairs.

ABOUT THE AUTHOR

Michael Z. Lewin was born in Springfield, Massachusetts, raised in Indianapolis, and graduated from Harvard in 1964. Before he wrote his first five novels, *Ask the Right Question* (1971), *The Way We Die Now* (1973), *The Enemies Within* (1974), *Night Cover* (1976), and *The Silent Salesman* (1978), he taught in a New York City high school. He now lives with his wife and two children in Somerset, England, where his chief avocation is spreading the message of Indiana basketball.